He studied her in the darkness. "I would like to do that one New Year's Day. Share that sunrise with you."

As would she. Her cheeks warmed but the car was dimly lit. "Hard, if you live in Italy."

He didn't answer for a few seconds. "Indeed."

He opened his door and climbed out, and she pushed on her own. But, of course, he arrived to pull it wide and offer her a hand.

He took her fingers in his, looking down at her, not saying anything, and as she stood to balance herself, he tucked her hand under the crook of his elbow, drawing her closer than strictly required so that their hips touched.

His thigh was hard against her softer hip. She was well supported to keep from any hint of a stumble, but strangely her knees felt weak. Silly woman.

His warmth seeped into her.

As did the warmth flushing her chest.

His hand tightened and she lifted her chin to tilt her face up at him. For a moment she thought he was going to kiss her. The world stopped.

Dear Reader,

Welcome back to Lighthouse Bay for Dom and Isabel's story.

We met Isabel in *The Midwife's Secret Child*, where she was the sensible and stalwart aunt of Faith, and there was that moment when Isabel and Dom met at Faith's wedding that made me wonder if they were destined to be together.

Isabel believed she'd always be the aunt who was there for Faith, but now that her niece was married, what about her own life? Because she knew there was no chance of love for herself.

Dom, plagued by his tragic past, came from Florence for his twin brother's Australian wedding and planned to leave quickly. Except he found Isabel, a strong and insightful woman, who was happy to give him advice but brushed him off like an annoying lad when he provided his own. And yet she still captured his interest.

Taking a Chance on the Best Man is the story of two people who think they don't have enough to offer and the burst of bravery it takes to risk your heart. I hope you enjoy Dom and Isabel's story as much as I enjoyed the creation of these lovely people in the beautiful setting of Lighthouse Bay.

Xx *Fi*

TAKING A CHANCE
ON THE BEST MAN

FIONA McARTHUR

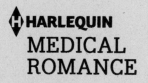

HARLEQUIN
MEDICAL
ROMANCE

HARLEQUIN®
MEDICAL ROMANCE™

Recycling programs
for this product may
not exist in your area.

ISBN-13: 978-1-335-40902-7

Taking a Chance on the Best Man

This edition published by arrangement with Harlequin Books S.A.

For questions and comments about the quality of this book, please contact us at CustomerService@Harlequin.com.

Harlequin Enterprises ULC
22 Adelaide St. West, 41st Floor
Toronto, Ontario M5H 4E3, Canada
www.Harlequin.com

Printed in U.S.A.

Fiona McArthur is an Australian midwife who lives in the country and loves to dream. Writing Medical Romance gives Fiona the scope to write about all the wonderful aspects of romance, adventure, medicine and the midwifery she feels so passionate about. When she's not catching babies, Fiona and her husband, Ian, are off to meet new people, see new places and have wonderful adventures. Drop in and say hi at Fiona's website: fionamcarthurauthor.com.

Books by Fiona McArthur

Harlequin Medical Romance

The Midwives of Lighthouse Bay

A Month to Marry the Midwife
Healed by the Midwife's Kiss
The Midwife's Secret Child

Christmas in Lyrebird Lake

Midwife's Christmas Proposal
Midwife's Mistletoe Baby

Gold Coast Angels: Two Tiny Heartbeats
Christmas with Her Ex
Second Chance in Barcelona

Visit the Author Profile page
at Harlequin.com for more titles.

Dedicated to my dear friend, Carolyn, who was there
for my first book and tragically gone for this one.
I will always feel a smile when I think of you and I bet
you're causing mayhem in heaven. xx Fi

**Praise for
Fiona McArthur**

"I absolutely adored the story…. Highly recommended
for fans of contemporary romance. I look forward to
reading more of Fiona McArthur's work."
—*Goodreads* on *Healed by the Midwife's Kiss*

CHAPTER ONE

JUST A WEEK since Domenico Salvanelli had first locked stares with her across the room and Isabel Fetherstone had been made inconveniently aware of a man seven years her junior. To make it even more awkward, there could be no doubt he was aware of her too.

Now, at her niece Faith's wedding rehearsal in Lighthouse Bay, Isabel tried to ignore the tingle in her fingers where they rested on the powerful forearm of the groom's twin.

Dom didn't smile, causing much concern to all, Isabel thought wryly, yet despite the angst emanating from him she thought of him as Dashing Dom. Couldn't help it. Though as the spinster aunt, fifteen years older than the bride, she'd never said Dom's pet name out loud. She'd sworn to be sensible, the one in control, and there was nothing controlled about such a delightful buzzing from a young man's steely arm.

Dashing Dom was a widower buried in grief

but before too long, like a male version of Sleeping Beauty, he would be in need of a new love.

He'd also be in need of a new Salvanelli heir. That ruled her out.

An heir sounded so old-fashioned—but there was the aristocratic old-world Italian culture of passing on gilded Florentine estates. Both brothers were ridiculously wealthy, and she had no doubt that they'd each want as many spares as possible.

As they walked together back up the aisle, best man and matron of honour, she tried not to inhale the particularly divine aftershave drifting next to her, or glance across at the impressive masculine chest stretched so delightfully close.

He made her feel a little wicked—almost as if they meant to brush against each other, invading mutual space—but they weren't. Or she wasn't. No, she couldn't accuse him of crowding, but his fierce concentration rippled her deep pond of serenity and made her aware of their proximity.

She wasn't one for flirting with toy boys, though the darkness behind his coal-black eyes belied naivety.

Secrets. Guilt. Baggage.

Dom had mountains of tormented baggage and the man would be high maintenance. But darn, he was pretty and made her blush.

Seriously, she wished she didn't find his gaze

on her every time she turned around, not saying anything, not helping her awareness. Watching her. As if he was trying to understand a divine puzzle.

As if she attracted him.

Again, ridiculous. Too young.

She didn't need a fling to divert her from this absolute highlight in her tiny family's life, if that was what he was trying to instigate. This was all about her niece Faith, who deserved the happiness she'd finally found with this man's brother. And Isabel was the sensible aunt. Always sensible. Always.

It was two days before the wedding breakfast in Lighthouse Bay and they stood in the church like puppets. And you know what? Weddings made her itch. Or they did with Dom beside her.

She thought about the last wedding she'd stood in as bridesmaid—her late sister's disaster—and promptly pushed away the memory of the desertion that husband had visited on his wife and daughter. And her own fiancé's desertion. Pushed them both far away.

Isabel had to believe Faith's marriage would be perfect because Faith and Rai were so much in love.

The groom and his brother—they were such uber males these Salvanellis—certainly knew how to convey dark and inscrutable, but now there was nothing mysterious about Rai. All she could see was blazing joy shining from that dear man's eyes. Isabel smiled warmly at him.

Beside her, Domenico leant in, his scent swirling like fine aromatic spice in a souk's dark alley. 'Why—?' he started, before another instruction from the jolly Catholic priest cut him off.

'We will start again,' the priest interjected. The Father had driven in from a nearby town to preside over the non-denominational chapel for the real event. And he wanted everything right.

Obediently, Dom closed his beautiful mouth, spun on his heel and returned to the altar to stand beside his brother. They restarted the rehearsal.

Isabel compressed her lips to hide her smile. Ah, Dom. Like a good Catholic boy, she thought, amused that he'd been thwarted, and trying not to flashback to the way his toned backside was cupped by his dark trousers as he stalked back.

'I think he likes you,' Faith's voice teased as Isabel took her arm to wait for their signal to begin another stately bridal walk.

'Who? Father Paul?' Teasing back. With a tinge of pride Isabel noted how calm and unfazed her niece had remained as her wedding day galloped towards them. A month wasn't long to arrange a wedding. Especially just before Christmas.

Isabel, acting also as the one to give away the bride, had no doubt Faith would be happy in marriage because these star-crossed lovers had waited a long time to rediscover each other. Five years of misunderstandings and interference from others. Enough time had been wasted. Now their future beckoned with wide open arms.

Faith pulled a non-bridal face. 'No, silly, not the priest. Dom fancies you.'

'Ah, that's what you mean.' As she smiled she hoped the twitch didn't look as false as it felt. Isabel tried not to think about that one time she too had thought she'd found true love. Or the man who'd left her when it was discovered how unlikely it would be for her to bear his child.

Or even, since then, on how she'd missed out on love completely by being the one in control, pulling back as soon as any man looked like being attracted to her.

This was Faith's wedding and she loved Faith, and her daughter Chloe, very much. She would do nothing to jeopardise that love. Certainly not come on to the groom's brother in a fit of ill-suited attraction.

'Dom is too young for me,' Isabel said, sounding calm as she and Faith waited together in the arched entrance for their next instruction. 'And we all know he has issues.'

Faith tossed her hand in the direction of her soon-to-be brother-in-law. 'You know how to deal with issues. You're the most level-headed person I know.' A waggle of eyebrows. 'And he's gorgeous.'

Yes, he was. 'You think he's hot because he looks like your husband-to-be.' But she couldn't stop the heat creeping up her cheeks. Just as her gaze crept up the long lines of Dom's body as he stood straight, tall and well-muscled beside his brother.

'True. But...' the bride's eyes strayed to her man '... Rai is hotter.' Faith's gaze came back to rest on Isabel's face. She studied her, unexpected glee in her eyes. 'I've never seen you blush before.' Her brows creased.

Suddenly thoughtful, her eyes became piercing. More serious. 'When that hunky locum doctor asked you out last week you weren't flustered,' she mused.

That man had been Isabel's age. Good-looking. Well-adjusted. Eminently suitable. And he hadn't interested her enough to accept a free dinner. She wondered if she would have said yes to Dom. Which was ridiculous. Disastrous. And a little scary.

For Isabel, the next few minutes were blessedly question-free, until she floated back down the aisle with Domenico's hot, corded muscles taut beneath her fingers. *Sigh*.

This time they strolled more companionably towards the exit, with the rehearsal ceremony finally concluded and only the practice waltzes to complete.

'Isabel,' he began again, his strong accent stretching the word out as if stroking her name with his long, strong fingers. 'Why are you not married?'

Why the heck did men say that to her? As if the world revolved around women lucky enough to find a man. Oh, she could find one. Just didn't trust them. Look at her sister's marriage. And her own broken engagement.

His comment made her impatient. 'I choose not to be.' She arched her brows at him. 'You've been a widower for six years. Why haven't you remarried?' She knew as soon as she'd said it she shouldn't have. It was an indication of how much this man unsettled her, and so unlike her to respond less than kindly. And he had so much angst.

She'd guarded her heart so well, been so independent, and now this young stranger addled her brain! Scattered her wits. Where was her level head now?

Dom's face darkened. 'I doubt I will ever re-marry.'

The words were accompanied by such a look of despair she wanted to shake him. For good-ness' sake! She got that he was heartbroken, and to lose a child would be the worst thing in the world—the absolute worst—but six years was a long time to grieve, feel guilt and grow old. She knew that. She'd done it for more than twice that and for the first time in all that time she wondered if she'd been a fool.

Dom should not be a fool. Especially if he had the ability to father another child. 'You're a young man.'

'I have been blessed once. And I failed to protect them.'

Guilt. Isabel knew about guilt. Especially un-founded guilt. Faith had told her his wife and child had been killed in a horrific balloon ride accident and that Dom had not gone with them on the day because of work. But too much guilt was harming this man. It harmed everyone. They all knew that.

The priest had followed them out and he smiled as he came towards them. Isabel dropped Dom's arm. 'Yet you have a dynasty to pass on.' She looked at the cleric.

'Father Paul, I always thought that God's

plans could not be understood by mere mortals.' She felt Dom stiffen beside her.

The priest smiled benignly at them. 'So true. Repentance brings peace and new beginnings. Guilt and shame and blame have no place in God's world.' He waved his hand up at the heavens and floated away to speak to the bridal couple like a whimsical white-frocked cloud. Leaving an anvil of emotion in storm cloud Dom.

He rose to his full height, towering over her. His face a mask, transitioned to a hardness she hadn't seen before. Impressive. She'd obviously struck a nerve and the priest had been a little more on the knocker than she'd bargained for.

'I lost my wife. And my son.' His face came closer. Very softly he continued, 'You, a spinster who eschews marriage, you have not had a child. You do not understand.'

At Dom's words her breath caught somewhere under her ribs, sharp and stabbing, as a wave of long-checked agony burst through her like a knife. Lacerating. Lancing her. Licking with pain.

'That's true.' Almost. She'd never married and she'd lost a baby, not a child. Only Faith knew. This was a secret she didn't share, not even with her closest friends.

Dom's stab in the dark had drawn blood. Touché. Hers had too.

Few knew of the stillbirth, nor of its aftermath, when she'd been told her uterus was misshapen and an inhospitable place for pregnancy. She'd tucked that away in her deep, dark, sorrow-filled soul, desperate for a child of her own.

She'd been stupid to comment. Stupid to ask the priest to comment. Now, forcing calm, she lifted her eyes to the man by her side. She looked right into his tortured eyes and said, 'I'm sorry for your loss.'

She walked away.

Two days later, at the front of the church, Dom's face felt hard like the painted granite around him as he stared inscrutably ahead in his matching black suit. It was difficult, in this time of joy for his brother, not to think of his own tragic marriage and the loss of his family. And when he did think of new beginnings, as his twin had suggested so often, then guilt chewed at him like a carnivorous beast.

'Brother?' Dom turned to look at Rai as he spoke, and some of the strain eased away. 'Today is for rejoicing, yes?'

'Indeed.' His twin was in love. *Amore*. Domenico felt his mouth kink upwards. 'I rejoice.

You managed to wait a whole month before you married your Faith.'

Rai laughed quietly. 'It was not possible for more speed or it certainly would have been sooner. Thank you for being here.'

He had only just made it. It had been difficult to extricate himself from the many technicalities of an incinerated business, and a lethargy steeped in despair had slowed him even more, but he had known he would have to come if Rai married in Australia.

He had to sympathise with his brother on the irresistible attraction of the Fetherstone women. Sadly, his brother had noted how Faith's aunt, Isabel, had caught his eye as well.

At the wedding rehearsal Isabel had brushed off Domenico's attention as if she were the older, wiser woman fussed over by a boy. It had been amusing to Rai, Dom knew, when Isabel was only seven years the elder and yet he had been markedly ruffled by her dismissal.

His reluctance to leave Florence when matters were urgent meant he'd had every intention of hurrying home as soon as the nuptials were completed. Though, to Rai's delight, it had taken just a few days in the company of Isabel Fetherstone for Domenico to mention to his brother that he might stay 'perhaps a little longer'.

After the briefest of honeymoons, Rai and Faith would return here to live. Lighthouse Bay, where the sea breeze blew through the open windows of the houses along with the noisy crashing of waves.

This bay, this place, held magic the like of which Dom had never felt before.

He glanced over his shoulder to see Faith's friends and colleagues in the congregation. They had already become Rai's associates. Though his brother might fly home many times, he doubted he would leave his new family behind or stay away from this place for long.

A car pulled up outside. Doors opened and his brother drew a deep breath beside him, impatient for his bride.

Dom too leaned forward.

The music started and a rustling at the door and a shift of light drew all eyes to the entrance.

Ah. The little flower girls. His niece Chloe like a daffodil in her sunshine-yellow dress, the lilac sash so pretty, her dark hair plaited around her sweet, serious face as she solemnly sprinkled yellow rose petals down the aisle for the bride. A little girl followed her, her own basket of dewy softness on her arm as she copied her friend. They looked like fairies as their glowing faces spread joy like the petals among the congregation.

Isabel stepped into view, head up, large eyes excited, yet her face was serene, her mouth curved in the happiness of the moment, and Dom tensed beside his brother. *Sì*, she was a vision.

Faith's aunt waited, stepped sideways, the maid of honour who refused to be bridesmaid. The pale lilac dress highlighted the dark auburn of her hair, the silk that slid and slithered over the slim body was modest but with that hint of allure his twin had found in Faith. And Dom had found in Isabel.

Isabel's face rose as the music lifted to a climax and the bride stepped alone into the doorway. Then she reached out and rested her hand lightly on Isabel's arm.

Isabel would give the bride away for safe keeping, into the arms of the man she loved, as he had been told she would.

What was Isabel's story? Dom needed to know.

The reception was held at the surf club and after the photographs the bride and groom entered to the fun strains of a modern love song while the guests clapped and cheered. Isabel followed with Dom and the children, and she smiled at the happiness as Faith and Rai waltzed their way around the room smiling at each other. It was so beautiful to keep the momentum and excitement going.

Except now Isabel would have to dance with Dom when they joined the newlyweds in the centre of the room.

She could do this.

Isabel waited, her feet shifting on the wooden boards of the surf club with her fingers lost in Dom's large, firm hand as the first song ended and the slower waltz began.

Faith beckoned them to join.

Dom's other hand eased against the skin of her back, just above her buttocks, burning through the thin fabric of her dress as he pressed her into a closed stance. Standing there, so close, the scent of him was like rolling wine around in a glass and tasting. Delicious, flavoursome, intriguing. Darn him.

She felt tiny in Dom's arms. Feminine. Fluttery. It was certainly foolish to feel such things, but today was for celebration. For joy. For a little abandon.

The music began—*oom-pah-pah, oom-pah-pah, oom-pah-pah*—as Dom stepped sideways, leading her with a firmness and grace that, of course—cruel universe—she'd always searched for in a dance partner and never found. Typical.

Her lilac dress slithered against her skin; his arms were solid steel bands and perfectly positioned to allow her to flow with the music, an invitation to immerse herself, and she couldn't help the tiny smile. Letting herself go should have been harder with Dom. But she loved to dance and her hand on his shoulder unconsciously softened into trust.

He glanced down, his gaze intent on her expression, and though nobody could call it a twinkle in his eyes there was some kindlier emotion than some they had shared.

His mouth bent close. 'You dance well in my arms, Isabel.' The warmth of his breath stole a fragment of her composure and she would have stumbled if he hadn't had such control over them both. Perhaps his gaze held a touch of complacency that he knew she wasn't immune to his nearness. Yes, he could sense that her body responded to the feel of being held in his steady embrace. She could give him that. But his words implied that he had control. Not so.

She might be aware of his heat, his big body and his masculine scent but she wouldn't lose herself, throw good sense to the wind and let him dance her off to wherever he wanted. She wouldn't. Even if the idea had delightful merit.

A sensible woman wouldn't be feeling these things. But she couldn't help the softening of her body. The loss of herself to the step and sway in time to Dom's direction, clever, masterful dancer that he was.

The *oom-pah-pah* of the dance thrummed through her senses and his arms were so easy to glide in. She turned her face so he couldn't see her expression.

'Good,' he said. 'I will not let you fall.'

No. He wouldn't. Intrinsically she knew that. But she might. Fall. Fall for him. She understood the danger with a fear that was unlike anything she'd felt before. What was it about this man that called to the impulsiveness she'd denied for so long?

It was closing her throat. Speeding her heart until sense talked her down again. *It's just a dance.*

And it should be fun. This was a joyous occasion.

Why not let her hair down and enjoy these moments in an excellent dancer's arms?

'Can you be impulsive, Isabel?' His question startled her, the train of conversation so close to her own thoughts.

No. Yes. Could she?

Isabel tilted her chin at him. 'Of course.'

'Then do it.' He bent his face sideways. 'Let us enjoy the moment.'

He was right, darn him. Consciously she eased the remaining tension in her shoulders, loosened her grip and allowed him to lead more fully. Allowed herself to be whirled away. The guy could dance and she rarely had the chance. She lifted her face and smiled into his eyes. Impulsive behaviour had been absent from her life for so long.

Other couples joined them. Isabel immersed herself in the moment and swayed and spun again and let herself be held in this man's arms and savour it. To be rash.

Her mouth curved wider as she smiled up at him. The music soaked into her. His arms held her firmly, strongly leading them, his feet perfectly in time with hers. She could do this, have fun with this serious, seriously handsome young man. Her nephew by marriage.

The music stopped, yet for a moment they moved on—until Dom slowed and then stepped away, his hand sliding from her back.

She blinked and pulled her fingers down from his shoulder to clasp her other hand in front of herself. Her smile faded as she returned to the real world.

'Thank you for the dance,' she said quietly.

'We will do this again.'

His words made her nervous, but she pretended they didn't. It was just a dance. Fun. Nothing deep and meaningful. And he'd be going soon.

Isabel tucked her oddly trembling fingers against the sides of her pretty dress and looked around. Saw tables of happy people. The wedding breakfast served. Saw something that made her brows crease with concern.

She crossed to the older woman, Mrs Cross—a stalwart of the Ladies Auxiliary at the hospital—who normally enjoyed non-stop conversation, yet clutched her throat with shaky fingers. Her shorter, rounder husband hovered and waved at Isabel.

Isabel avoided a dancer as she neared their table in a few fast strides. 'Is everything okay?'

'Cynthia doesn't want to spoil the wedding.' Mr Cross's whisper was oddly strident. 'Won't let me tell anyone.'

His wife hushed him.

'What's wrong?' Isabel could tell something wasn't right. Mrs Cross's face seemed ringed with red and her neck had welts rising as Isabel watched. Allergy? 'Did you eat something that doesn't agree with you?' Isabel had had a friend with severe allergies; she knew about the dangers.

The older lady nodded forlornly at her plate. 'I think the salmon.' Her voice sounded hoarse and cracked. 'I love salmon. I'm not allergic to the salmon, just prawns. But now I'm not sure.

My lips feel funny and numb.' She coughed. 'And I'm having trouble breathing.'

'She has a needle for prawns.' Mr Cross patted his pockets and pulled out a silver case which opened to reveal the plastic barrel of an EpiPen. 'But she's never been allergic to salmon before.'

Epinephrin? Isabel felt her heart thump. Serious allergy. She looked around for help without causing a scene, but everyone was watching the dancers. She caught Dom's eye; he was watching her.

She waved him over and took the pen from Mr Cross as his wife coughed. She knew about pens. This wasn't a good time to wait for the airway to close. She unwrapped the plastic from the barrel, flipped off the top cap, pushed the orange base against Mrs Cross's upper leg and pressed the pen into the side of her thick thigh until it clicked.

Dom arrived and took Mrs Cross's wrist in his hand. 'EpiPen,' she said. Their eyes met and he nodded.

'Waiting, one, two, three,' Isabel said to Mrs Cross then removed the needle. 'It's done. Nobody noticed. Let's slip you down to the hospital to get checked. Dr Salvanelli will come with us in your car; that will be faster than an ambulance.'

She knew the dose of epinephrine would boost Mrs Cross's falling blood pressure and reduce the swelling, but the older lady needed observation away from the wedding reception. Isabel suspected Faith's guest would have quickly progressed to full anaphylaxis if treatment hadn't been at hand, bless her husband.

Said husband had shakily pulled car keys from his other pocket and Dom and Isabel ushered the woman out of the door unobtrusively, taking her tottering weight between them until they could carefully help her into the car.

It was all over in moments. The drive down the hill. The stop at the hospital doors. Their charge handed over to the emergency staff.

A relieved Mr Cross refused to let them walk back up the hill and drove them back to the reception before turning his car again. They didn't talk on the drive, but Isabel mulled over the event.

Dom had been great. It was nice to have discreet medical backup, she thought. Someone who was quietly efficient. Calm. As she had been herself. And barely anyone had noticed the emergency, certainly not the bride and groom, much to Mrs Cross's relief. Isabel smiled at that.

They did have things in common.

And things that kept them apart.
And still that attraction.

Back at the reception, Faith and Rai came over
to them with puzzled looks on their faces. 'What
happened? Where did you go? It's time for the
speeches.'

Isabel and Dom silently agreed to play it
down. She let him talk. 'All is well, brother. I
will tell you later. Let us have speeches.'

Domenico Salvanelli watched his twin brother's
car disappear down the hill, his new wife at his
side. He saw them drive past the inflated, red-
suited St Nicholas who stood on, of all things
not holy, a surfboard at the end of the street.
Past the sign to the beach and the lighthouse.

Nine days since he had arrived in this sun-
drenched bay of white sand and strange, yet
compelling people on the coast of eastern Australia. And only five days until the day he
dreaded the most every year. Christmas—without his family. Which was why he was flying
out of this joyful place the day before the best
and worst memories of his life.

Yet since his arrival in Australia he was re-
alising he needed to change. The catalyst of the
factory burning down had left him at his low-

est but now, with his brother's wedding today, this place had seemed to halt the deadly slide.

He'd been existing not living since Teresa and Tomas had been lost, and suddenly there was this place. A vibrant place of sun and smiles.

And this amazing woman, Isabel, who had made him consider himself in a different light.

But still he held back.

For a moment the strangeness of standing here, half a world away from his home in Florence, overwhelmed him. In his home city frosty air would be rustling the huge decorated tree and nativity scene in Piazza del Duomo.

Here in Australia it burned hot and strange and Santa had replaced Saint Nicholas. He couldn't see a single manger, though Chloe, his brother's newly discovered five-year-old daughter, had told him there were such to be found. He couldn't see even a Wise Man in a garden.

But women? Perhaps he had found a wise woman. He looked towards Isabel, so prudent and practical when he looked into her calm face. Yet, despite her composed neutrality towards him, in only these few days he'd realised she intrigued him more than any woman in years.

Isabel's understated beauty called to him. She rippled his previously frozen world like the warm sea wind tossed the dark riot of her hair around her face in soft strands. Her hair was like the woman, with hidden depths—a ruby in the depths, glowing like the heart of her. He wished to stroke the texture of both and discover if she were as soft as she looked.

He'd been in mourning for so long, the fact that suddenly this woman attracted him was shocking for him. How had he let her overtake his thoughts in this way? Was his brother right? Could he come to Australia with the idea of making a new start, perhaps? Was he in the perfect place and time to be attracted to someone new, even as this thought terrified him?

He'd tried to work out Isabel's attraction for him.

To see the charm of Isabel.

But it was no one thing.

She danced like an angel. Cared for all with her goodness. Yet spoke her thoughts without fear.

Her mind shone with flashes of brilliance and subtle strength—mostly disguised but never fully contained and deeply intriguing. The impenetrable wall she had erected between them made her unobtainable and even more desirable. He had not experienced such barriers before or after his loss of Teresa. And when had he been able to think of his wife without searing pain? He could not remember.

The recognition of a kindred soul had jolted

him at his first sight of Isabel. So much so he'd started in surprise. She'd shown no such discomfort. She rarely did. That fascinated and annoyed him, used as he was to his volatile and flamboyant countrymen and women in Italy.

Then he'd begun to notice other things. Her care and consistent compassion towards her niece Faith and great-niece Chloe, and her obvious approval and delight in his brother's love for Faith.

Rai had said this sensible woman had been a rock for his Faith and Chloe, and that Isabel held few prejudices.

Yet?

Towards him, he felt a strong prejudice. An annoying wall that made him want to ripple her serenity in retaliation for the confusion she left him feeling.

Between them some barrier stayed, contained and controlled and repelling even his most subtle advances. Yet he'd sensed from the beginning that there was a passionate woman underneath the façade, and he was drawn to that in her. Had sensed it from the dancing. Holding her in his arms had been a revelation. A joy. Almost an addiction.

But he couldn't understand why he thought so. Or why she was the one. It was as if an unexpected fairy tale had opened before him.

He thought of that conversation outside the church on the rehearsal day. She seemed to have forgotten, yet he regretted it every night in his bed. The memory had robbed him of sleep. He could still see her stricken eyes after he'd cruelly called her a spinster who would not understand.

He'd seen that quick flash of pained emotion, and yet she had sounded so calm. He remembered her response. 'That's true,' she'd said. 'I'm sorry for your loss.'

But he sensed a deep well of pain in this woman and knew he'd caused it. He wanted to know how and why.

He had apologised the next day. Yet she had waved off his apology as unnecessary. As if it hadn't mattered to her at all. But he wondered. Suspected. Doubted.

And earlier today, the moments when she'd taken control of the situation with the anaphylactic woman at the wedding as if it was not worthy of comment, which for a layperson it surely was. Yet when he'd asked she'd brushed that away too, mentioned a friend. He didn't understand Isabel. But he wanted to.

Today, watching her niece drive away with his brother, their child's fingers clinging to hers, the intriguing angles of Isabel's face drew him again. That and her quietude. She was like an island haven in a sea of tempests. While he was a raging sea of conflicting emotions.

Turning her lithe body towards Chloe, he saw Isabel gently squeeze the little girl's hand. When her gaze lifted to his it was as if she sensed his melancholy. He forced a smile, avoided her all-seeing green eyes and looked at Chloe.

Chloe's lips quivered, her face pinched, and her free hand reached to dash away the glint of tears from her cheek as the car bearing her parents disappeared from sight.

For Dom, a surge of renewed pain of loss for his own wife and child pierced him with familiar despair. Six years. And yet in the last year he'd seemed to be grieving more deeply as time went on, not less. It was an illness that needed treatment, or a great change in his life, his brother kept saying.

He turned from the child. He needed to go home to Florence. This place unsettled him.

'Let's have pizza tonight for dinner, Chloe.' Isabel's calm, pleasing voice carried to him as he began to walk away.

'Do you like pizza, Uncle Domenico?' a piping, uncertain voice spoke to his back. The forlornness in the words froze his movement. It called to him, penetrated his own misery.

He had felt like that. Bereft.

He turned and saw the worried frown of his

little niece, so unexpectedly like his own dear mamma's face and yet not, and dragged himself from the past.

His son Tomas, barely two years older than this child when he had died, had loved pizza. But Tomas was gone, as was his Teresa, and his brother had dragged him here to his new family across the sea for the next few days. He needed to lift himself and pretend he didn't want to join his own family in death, forget that he'd been spiralling this past year into a darkness he felt he could not escape.

'*Sì*.' He straightened his shoulders and forced another smile. 'But your papa has a new special oven in his house. I could make us all pizzas when the last of the workmen go home. Would you like that?'

The constant clatter of tradesmen from the tall dwelling across the street ceased at five in the afternoon until seven the next morning. The whole renovation would be completed soon, when his brother and his new wife returned from their brief honeymoon.

Then finally, just before Christmas, Dom would fly home.

'Can I help make them?' Chloe's eyes were imploring and only a sterner man than he would have been able to deny her.

He looked at his new relation by marriage for

permission. Isabel nodded, though he couldn't tell if she was pleased that they would now join him for the evening meal. Her composure was a pleasant mask he wished to remove with a growing desire, but the key eluded him. She was like the lighthouse across the bay. Eye-catching, standing tall and watchful. But locked.

'Your aunt says yes. So *sì*.' He nodded. 'First I must go down to the shops and buy a few items. But I will call for you when I am ready to begin the preparations.' It would give him something to do. He hadn't cooked for years. The child made him smile. Something else he hadn't done for years.

And Isabel would be there. Perhaps he would learn something about her. The idea excited him in unfamiliar ways. He might discover something more than the few scant details she had shared so far and, if he was careful, perhaps he could penetrate the shield she held between them. And, in doing so, was there hope for restoration of their rapport and even, down the road, more than friendship?

Isabel drew Chloe towards their gate—her gate, now she had taken over the freehold ownership, with all of Chloe and Faith's belongings tucked into the new built-in wardrobes and drawers across the road in the Captain's house. She still

smiled when she thought about Rai's impulsive
purchase of the imposing turreted building the
day he'd discovered his daughter. And the re-
lentless renovations that had ensued since then.

The Captain's house stared haughtily over the
roof of her own small dwelling. But her windows gazed across the blue waves of the inlet to
the tall white tower on the oceanside cliff face
that gave the town its name. Lighthouse Bay.

She could not imagine Dashing Dom being
as impulsive as his brother. But damaged men
were rarely impulsive, unless in the worst way
possible.

Of which Rai had warned her.

Dom's endless despair, guilt. And pain.

The thought made her cold.

She understood why mental illness drew people to remove unbearable suffering for ever. Yet
during this morning's wedding there had been
moments when she had seen the man Rai had
assured her was inside his brother. He had so
much to be proud of.

The dapper best man. So tall and handsome.

The delightful dancer who'd smiled into her
eyes and held her during the bridal waltz.

The doctor, there when she'd needed him earlier today.

Despite herself she'd wished he were a decade
or two older, past the age of wanting children,

so that she could act on the spine-tingling attraction she still fought. And do something for him that proved life was for living. Her cheeks warmed and she looked down at her hands. *Tsk, Isabel, when did you last think about seduction?* The thought sent a low, tickling warmth through her belly and she squashed the excitement it brought. Darn shame indeed.

No! Stop.

The last thing this man needed was to become fond of her until she stepped away. Heaven knew he needed a young, fertile wife to give him many children. Men were capable of fathering well into middle age, while she wasn't capable of childbearing at all.

Isabel had never been one to allow herself torment over what she couldn't have. Or, when it arose, the fact that others could, so easily. Like when her niece hadn't intended to fall pregnant over five years ago with Rai. Because the result was Chloe, a gift for all of them.

Certainly she didn't anguish over young men, out of bounds not only because of the age difference but because they had empires to pass on. And they were related by marriage. Isabel considered herself blessed to have shared the upbringing of her dear older sister's daughter and later Chloe. Her own loss had been eased by that sharing.

She was happy being the favourite aunt—so happy with that. She had a job she loved—not the midwifery she'd once practised but hadn't been able to face after her own fertility issues were discovered, but as part-time receptionist at the hospital—and was involved in many of the small town's social clubs and charity works. Life was good. Men asked her out—some young, some not so—but she rarely went twice. That way she had no need to explain her dysfunction as a woman if someone began to care.

Her rules. Though now she had passed forty she could look at older men with no wish for children in a more permanent way. Strangely, the ones she seemed to meet just didn't feel right.

Thankfully, this next year she would return to her travel and try to resurrect her contacts she'd made in the travel writing industry before Chloe had been born.

Freedom again. She wasn't needed now, superfluous.

Faith's needs had changed: she was married with a husband, and Chloe had found her lost father.

Isabel's travel writing and photographs had been sought after in the past and would be again.

With the changes in Faith's life came changes in Isabel's. New opportunities, including the chance to return to her great love: travel. Life was good and soon, she decided, it would be even better.

CHAPTER TWO

Dom began the preparations for the evening meal and shook his head in wonder. Who would imagine a device to slice vegetables could give so much pleasure, both to the user and the observers? Dom thought, still surprised at his own enjoyment.

He'd found the gadget in the tiny supermarket and had hoped it would protect his young niece's fingers from the need to use a knife.

His gaze met Isabel's over the top of the small head that bent so industriously over the chopping board. He smiled at her and she smiled back, one of the most delightful acknowledgements he'd had. Except for the dancing.

She looked away. He did too. Back at Chloe.

One small hand gripped the protective cover of the chopper, fiercely anchoring it to the wooden board, while the other stiffly spread palm beat violently down on the spring-loaded top in a deafening rata-tat-tat. In rapid slices the

blades within the clear dome dissected the vegetables holding the shards captured.

When the green pieces were almost too small
he said, 'Bravo, Chloe. Your capsicum is perfect.'

'Heh-heh-heh.' The short, satisfied chortle
from the child—very much like the wicked
witch's cackle in some fantasy film, he thought—
made him laugh out loud. The sound from his
throat was unfamiliar and he glanced up to see
the amused raised brows of the woman opposite.

He gestured with his hand. 'Her laugh...'

'I know. Classic.' Isabel's amusement crinkled her face and more warmth flooded him.
Dom passed the little girl the thick ham on a
new board. Normally he would have torn it, but
watching her chop made all of them smile.

'I don't know why I haven't bought one of
those before,' Isabel murmured, shaking her head
at her niece. 'Perhaps for your next birthday?'

He was pleased with himself that he could
tell the lovely Isabel was joking. His new need
to impress and begin to know her excited him,
though Dom pretended this was not so, and only
inclined his head sagely. He held her gaze when
she swung it his way. 'There is much pleasure
to be had.' To his delight Isabel blushed and he
wondered if she too felt the pull between them,
the double meaning in his words.

'What else can I chop?' Chloe's eyes, sparkling emerald-green like a precious gem, showed all of her pleasure at their industry. She had her mother's eyes. And her aunt's. And why did his thoughts always end back at the aunt?

'Will you eat mushrooms?' Dom asked. He knew the fungi were often disliked by children.

Chloe wrinkled her nose and he suppressed his smile. She looked up, her eyes imploring for more to cut. 'I could chop mushrooms. Perhaps we could put them on one side only of the pizza if I share with Aunty Izzy?'

'We can do that,' Isabel said. She scooped away the capsicum onto a saucer and replaced it with a mushroom.

'My son Tomas did not like mushrooms either.' Dom stopped. He never ever spoke of Tomas. This was huge. Memories had been suppressed because of the pain. But just this once he spoke of him to his new niece Chloe, a flame of hope for the future, as all children were. And with Isabel, because of her kindness and understanding, it did not seem too bad; it seemed almost natural. In sharing a memory he experienced such a feeling of relief to let the words out.

Chloe paused her cutting and small arched brows drew together as her eyes met his. The child's regard seemed wise beyond her five years. 'Mummy said Tomas and his mamma died before I was born.' Before he could say anything she went on. 'My nana died too. And sometimes Mummy or Aunty Izzy say I'm like her. Was Tomas like you?'

He swung his face to Isabel, expecting her to stop the child speaking of loss. She didn't. She smiled. Perhaps ruefully or perhaps with some expectation that he would answer.

Dom found himself closing his eyes at the remembered inquisitiveness of a child. The sudden sweetness of faith that the adult would know all the answers.

'*Sì*. He was like me. And like his Uncle Raimondo.'

'My papà.' She nodded sagely. The silence lengthened. Her lips parted in a smile. 'Can I chop cheese now, please?'

He pulled his emotions back under control. Moistening dry lips with his tongue, he spread his hands. 'Sadly, I have cheese already grated.' Ridiculously, he was sorry he had not chosen a block that Chloe could dissect. 'But you could have tomatoes to attack. And then basil.'

An hour later, Isabel sat well-sated with pizza, hers with lots of mushrooms, on the upstairs veranda.

The view lay before them on the outdoor first-floor space. Across the street her own house perched below through the wrought-iron railing and then across the bay, past the lighthouse and out to sea, the view swept on. Chloe's new father had purchased a telescope with a wheeled base and steps for the one cupolaed turret so she could watch ships on the ocean and imagine adventurous quests. Faith had said already the turret was a frequent hideaway for Chloe. They'd all looked through the telescope and Isabel had been surprised how clear the view had been.

For Isabel, this time with Dom and Chloe had been an evening of pleasant surprises. The man had been different, almost social at times.

Small pleasures. And not just the delicious food.

'Does it snow in Florence at Christmas? Like the North Pole?' Chloe rested her chin on one small hand as she watched her big uncle sip his tea.

Surreptitiously, Isabel watched him too. Dark brows. Espresso eyes. Sensuous lips. She watched as he sipped and felt her skin warm. Pulled her eyes away. It seemed he'd acquired the taste for their favourite green ginger tea, judging by the satisfied way he put his cup down. That surprised her, this big man enjoying caffeine-free tea. But then he'd surprised her a lot this evening.

The sea breeze stirred a swirl of dark hair across his high forehead, the shadows of the evening making the sharp lines and angles of his aristocratic face smoother. Less grim and forbidding than the normal frown which seemed habitual.

'It does not snow often in Firenze.' He looked at Chloe to explain. 'That is the Italian word for Florence.'

The little girl nodded. Rai had been teaching her some Italian words so she understood the concept.

They'd decided not to turn the lights on as night crept in on them, but she could see enough to know his face had softened for real at Chloe's question.

'Turin, in the north, is a place people go to see reliable snow and to ski on the mountains. In December, Turin has its annual Luci d'Artista, where the city and its people light up buildings and artworks in wonderful ways. Your papà would no doubt take you there to show you if you asked him.'

'That sounds nice.' Chloe wasn't interested in Turin or the festival, Isabel could tell, but Isabel most certainly was. She would love to visit again…had revelled in the cobbles of the streets, the red of the flowers and the history of villages tucked away on the hills. Yes. She could go back.

'I've never seen snow,' Chloe said thoughtfully. Her head swung towards her aunt, dark plaits swishing in the air. 'Have you seen snow, Aunty Izzy?'

'Yes. And I have even been to Turin in December. It is very beautiful. I will show you my photographs tomorrow if you like.'

Chloe nodded before continuing on her quest for more personal knowledge. 'Have you been to Florence? Where Papà and Uncle Domenico lived?'

Isabel smiled. She had the feeling that Chloe had beaten Dom to the question.

Dom sat forward as if interested.

'Where your uncle lives now? Yes. Another beautiful city.'

'Firenze is *the* most beautiful city,' Dom corrected, his voice a deep rumble in the night, almost teasing, his dark-as-night eyes intense on her face. Deep in her belly she could feel that smoulder of forgotten rolling, pulsing heat flicker into flame. For goodness' sake, had it really been more than a decade since she'd fancied a man? It might be time to go home, away from the warmth in his gaze. Back to safety.

As if totally unmoved, Isabel recalled herself to Dom's statement and agreed. 'I admit to a special charm in Florence, yes.'

'Pah!' he murmured in pretended disgust. 'Firenze is not charming; she is a gilded, glorious goddess of a city, with great beauty and wondrous art.'

That made her laugh. All he needed to do was to stand and throw out his arms. He was like a small boy who had been disagreed with. 'She is.'

His gaze shifted and caught hers. 'You should come to Florence. When Rai brings his bride.'

Good grief. She tried to break the link. 'And why would I do that?'

He shrugged those massive shoulders.

She arched her brows as if not understanding. 'I'm minding Chloe for their three-day honeymoon in Queensland. The rest they will do as a family.'

'But if we left when they returned? The whole family, including you, could have Christmas in Florence instead of the newlyweds waiting here for the festive season to pass. They could take their time, stay longer in Italy with just the two travelling at first, knowing Chloe was in the same country with you.'

Domenico's voice rumbled, low and persuasive, beside her. Were they to have Christmas in an aircraft flying over the ocean? She imagined

Chloe's disgust, let alone Chloe seeing her parents disappear to have fun. Isabel glanced sideways with mild amusement at him. 'And what would Chloe and I do while waiting in Florence during their initial grand tour?'

'There is much to see.' He lowered his head until his eyes met hers and, though he didn't truly smile, his chocolate eyes darkened and the corner of his mouth rose minutely with a sensual slant. It was quite shocking after all the serious faces and grim expressions she'd seen from him until now.

Mentally Isabel stepped back. He was too darn attractive for someone she wasn't encouraging, but those sexy insights this gorgeous man threw her way left her belly warm and her toes wanting to curl. It was most inconvenient to say the least.

'Funny you think that.' Now she sipped her own tea and continued sipping, pause, sip, until she had herself under control. 'I'm sure Rai is happy to spend time with his newly discovered daughter. And Faith has never been without her.'

'Of course. He is besotted with the child.' He waved his hand again, a more open smile tugging at his lips as he glanced at the young girl in question, who had stood to look at a ship from another viewpoint. 'I too find the child delightful. I would show you both around, of course.'

He wiggled a big hand as if saying could she not see the idea of the parents wanting to be alone for some time?

Isabel laughed. She hadn't thought he had it in him. Nice to know he wasn't all doom and gloom and tortured looks. 'Thank you for the invitation. But I am happy to agree with what Faith has decided on.'

'Do you not follow the impulse? Do what *you* wish?' His dark brows drew together solemnly, as if sad for her. There was emphasis on the *you*.

In return, she smiled sweetly and turned away to look at the view. 'I can be impulsive. And I always do what I wish. When I decide. I'm determined. Right now, it's time for Chloe to go to bed.'

Chloe piped up, 'I was in hospital.'

'And that was not too long ago.' She turned to Dom. 'I'm sure your brother mentioned Chloe had a secondary immune response and low blood counts that left her very ill. Time for bed.' Isabel stood and of course, as she'd expected, Dom stood immediately in response. 'We shall say goodnight to your uncle and thank him for the pizza.'

'Thank you for the pizza, Uncle Domenico.' Chloe stretched out his name again, to ensure she had it correct.

He smiled at her. 'Perhaps it would be easier to say Uncle Dom.'

'Yes.' Chloe breathed out a sigh of relief. 'Uncle Dom,' she repeated and stepped forward to throw her arms exuberantly around him.

Isabel saw Dom close his eyes for a moment as if in pain and then his big hands came down to the young girl's shoulders and he hugged her to him. 'Goodnight, little one.' He released her and looked across at Isabel. 'Thank you for the company.'

'And you for your hospitality,' she said and, despite her intention to remain cool, she couldn't help the flash of amusement that spread through her as she remembered Chloe's endeavours in the kitchen. 'I must buy a vegetable dicer.'

'Yes.' He inclined his head, his eyes twinkling, and she was glad his mood had lightened with Chloe's company.

'Goodnight.'

'Goodnight, Isabel. Perhaps you too could shorten my name?'

'Perhaps.' But she didn't say Dom. Because that would be the first admission that his name left her feeling flustered and feminine and fluttering like a moth under his bright gaze.

Not that she was afraid to use his name out loud. Was she? No.

'I will walk you across the street.' He held the

veranda door open for them to enter the house and go down the stairs.

Chloe skipped through and Isabel murmured as she passed, 'You could watch from here.'

'But I will come nevertheless.' His words were low and determined and not quite close enough to brush her neck as he stepped in after them. Her skin tingled as if he had and she remembered the dances they'd shared. His breath in her ear. His arms hot and hard. His thigh against hers.

'I've travelled the world on my own.' *Darn sexy man,* Isabel thought. *I can manage to get across a street in my own town.* But, because she was supposed to be the sensible, composed woman everyone thought her, she didn't say that. Coolly, she hoped it looked that way as she walked ahead of him to follow her niece out of the door.

True to his word, he followed them across the road and to their gate.

'Goodnight,' she said again. But she still didn't say his name. Although she rolled it silently around in her mind.

She could have said his name, Dom thought with unexpected irritation. Or turned around to look at him as she closed the door quietly.

Not as if he wasn't standing outside watching them walk away.

He turned and strode under the streetlights downhill towards the beach, his footsteps sounding a little too forcibly on the footpath. The salty breeze lifted the hair around his face and blew back the collar of his shirt to cool his neck in the ridiculous heat of December.

Christmas. Weddings. Small children. All things he dreaded. And yet his heart felt lighter than it had in a long time, a frisson of excitement piercing the darkness of his soul—though admittedly with some exasperation for the nonchalance of the woman he had just left. The woman who unsettled him.

He swivelled his head and looked at the unfamiliar festive lights. It was the place that unsettled him. So different from home. Not Isabel causing him to be disconcerted.

The beach came into sight with the moon climbing from the waves to the sky. Yes, his brother's new hometown was a beautiful place. And it had beautiful women residing in it. Or at least one beautiful woman.

He laughed grimly. He should have gone home straight after the wedding, but Rai had asked him to stay so that the bride might feel even more at ease leaving her daughter for the three nights.

As Isabel had said, Chloe had been ill recently and he was a doctor, if not practising often. The demands of the pharmaceutical company had been all-consuming, but his credentials were still there. Used rarely, at his brother's urging.

But watching over his daughter had not been Rai's only reason for asking him to stay. He knew Rai had been worried about him.

About the darkness Dom held inside. His state of mind. His intentions for the future.

Dom stood on the edge of the sand, looking out over the ocean where waves collided and smashed, and was suddenly glad the swirling water held no attraction to walk towards the horizon until the water closed over his head.

His brother was right. He did need to make a life change. Find joy in small things that had eluded him for too long.

His grandfather's factory, the millstone that had once saved his sanity in his hour of need, was gone, recently lost in flames and destruction, with reams of red tape all that was left if he wished to rebuild someone else's dream. It was the reason he had to leave Lighthouse Bay very soon and fly home or the family would lose the opportunity to rebuild.

It had never been his dream, more a deathbed promise he'd gladly been buried under after

Teresa and Tomas had died. With the recent fire and destruction, the excuse to block out the world with his grandfather's legacy had also been left in ruins.

He had no focus. No goal to strive for. No desire or duty to drive him to rebuild something he had never felt passionate about. But there were many legal and financial responsibilities he needed to complete speedily when he returned, before the end of the month or the permits would expire. He'd let things come to such a pass with his lowered mood.

This morning Rai had suggested he return here once his business was completed, that they open a general medical practice together in Lighthouse Bay. A trial of one year. It had been the first mention of the subject, to be discussed later.

He'd been astounded. Had denied the possibility of a return to medicine. He was a pharmacist now. Had been in charge of his grandfather's pharmaceutical company for years.

Though perhaps it was not so astounding.

Of course, such a venture would involve further refreshment of his knowledge. He'd need more medical expertise than the work in Third World countries he had occasionally been drawn into when his brother had needed him.

Such a venture would also require that he

gained registration in another country, though in Italy his volunteer work had kept him legally registered.

But to move across the world? To this strange town on the edge of the ocean?

He would need to find a place of residence because he would not live with newlyweds.

His mouth lifted in a small smile. He doubted that Isabel would allow him to sleep with her in her house.

Madonna. His breath sucked in, held low and hot in his chest as he stared dumbfounded at the moon. Imagined himself in Isabel's bed. Had his attraction to Isabel gone so far? Had he forgotten his wife? His loss? His loyalty?

Six years.

His breath hissed out. Perhaps his fun-loving, tempestuous Teresa would not have expected life-long mourning from him; he wondered why for so long he had.

CHAPTER THREE

'Aunty Izzy, Aunty Izzy, there's a rainbow.'

The next morning Isabel woke to a cloudy sky with sunbeams piercing her windows.

A small child flew through the air to land on her bed. She pulled her feet to the side quickly to prevent toe squashing and made a space for Chloe to wriggle and bounce.

'A rainbow?' Her face stretched into a yawn and her hand came up to cover her mouth. 'Did it rain this morning?' She must have been more deeply asleep than she remembered. It had taken her so very long to sink into slumber, thanks to the irritating Italian next door. Libidinous thoughts were not the norm for her. Or conducive to rest. Good grief, she'd actually felt sexually frustrated last night in her bed.

Isabel turned her head to look from her niece to the window and, sure enough, prismed colour gleamed in a semi-circle to the left of the pane.

'Can we take a photo for Mummy?' A par-

ticularly energetic bounce on the bed made a
pillow hit the floor. 'And for my papà.' Chloe's
addition made Isabel smile. Chloe still wasn't
used to having that extra person in the family
but loved inserting 'my papà' into most conversations now.

Isabel sat up and pushed her hair from her
eyes. 'Of course.' She'd tried showing Chloe
ways to compose photographs and her niece
had been a precociously apt pupil. 'Though we
may have to find a good vantage spot to work
the whole rainbow in.' She slid from the bed and
absently grabbed the nearest pair of shorts, bra
and top and headed for the bathroom. 'You'd
best get dressed if we're going up the hill. We'll
have to be quick to catch the light.'

Chloe catapulted off the bed in a leap and
disappeared.

Five minutes later they slipped out of the front
door just as the tall, dark, brooding neighbour
across the road did the same. Isabel suppressed
a sigh. Darn it. She knew what would happen
now.

'Uncle Dom, Uncle Dom, there's a rainbow.
We're taking a photo for Mummy and my papà.
Will you come and find it with us?'

Yup. She'd known. And here she was, dressed
in her shortest gym shorts and a skimpy sin-

glet top. Not what she would have worn if she'd thought ahead sensibly; running into their neighbour was always a possibility in their quiet street.

Lack of sleep to blame. Nothing else.

Isabel lifted her chin. Closing the gate after the little girl, she looked up to smile calmly into the dark gaze of the man who had invaded her dreams most inconveniently. He was studying her in the thorough way of Italian men regardless of their age. He'd better keep his hands to himself or he'd lose them.

'Your timing is impeccable.' Her voice might have sounded a tad dry, so she softened it with another smile.

'*Sì.*' There might even have been an amused twinkle in the dark eyes. 'And there is a rainbow, I am told. May I join you?'

Isabel felt like saying '*Sì*, I have no choice.' But she didn't. 'Of course,' she said instead and smiled tranquilly.

The two adults followed the skipping, hopping, trotting girl up the hill, past the row of crofts on the right that clung to the edge of the cliff. As they walked past they could glimpse the magnificent views over the bay between the houses.

'Who lives there?' Dom's interest seemed significant and she felt a tiny disquiet at his question. Could he be looking for a property? She thought it unlikely he would imitate his brother, but she still didn't trust these Salvanelli men not to buy real estate on a whim.

Isabel pointed them out. 'My friend Myra and her husband Reg, and next door is Sam and Ellie, and next to them Finn and Trina. Midwives and their doctor husbands—all friends of Faith and Rai who you met at the wedding.'

'And friends of yours, of course?'

Funny. She always thought of them as Faith's friends. Like a younger sibling's friends. 'Yes, my friends too, but they're a younger crowd. I have more in common with Myra as an older woman past childbearing age.'

Now why the heck had she said that?

She wanted to turn around and walk back down the hill. She never ever talked like that. Maybe she could knock her head against the wall once she was safely inside her house in private. Why was she so insecure about her age, especially in relation to him? Why was she so convinced that he needed to produce an heir that it made their relationship impossible? He'd never actually said that to her. Indeed, it seemed her age didn't matter to him. What was holding her back?

Being comfortable alone? Lack of confidence that she could hold the attention of so young and virile a man? Fear that she would fall in love and he too would walk away?

She couldn't pinpoint it. But fear was there. No doubt about it.

This man unsettled her—made her blurt out the weirdest things—and she wasn't happy with herself.

But she couldn't abandon Chloe by scuttling off home. Instead, she increased her pace and tilted her head to stare pointedly at the rainbow. They passed the last house and the path widened to a seating area overlooking the bay.

'Here's a lovely spot to take the photo, Chloe. I think it's starting to fade so you'd better be quick.'

Isabel pulled her phone from the small bag she'd stowed it in, found the camera app and handed it to Chloe. 'Watch your horizons are level.'

Chloe took the phone carefully and began to take various angles, not just standing feet planted and front on. Isabel nodded in approval. 'Good girl. Nice composition.'

'She knows of photography?' He'd come up beside her while she'd been watching her niece and she inhaled that spicy scent he wore. Straight from the shower, she guessed, but she chose not to feel unwashed and underdressed. Not at all.

She needed a diversion. 'I'll buy her a camera soon. I believe children can learn camera basics very early. It seems a shame not to make the best of an opportunity to share knowledge. Rainbows are always fun to shoot.'

Dom tried not to stare at the long, strong and shapely legs and arms displayed in the micro shorts and thin-strapped top. It was difficult. *Dio*. Most difficult. There had been no instance in the last few days that Isabel had not been covered and demure. And this morning so much wonderful woman was on display that for the first time in many years he felt the hot surge of desire.

He guessed she'd left the house hurriedly for the child and the thought amused him. She would dislike that, though he didn't know how he could be so sure of it. But he was.

Sure and delighted.

Yet still she showed no outward sign of awareness of her attire. She was an unusual woman and Dom suspected that she sold herself short if the few years between her niece's friends and her own age seemed such a huge gap. Perhaps this Myra was of the same age.

He then considered if this mindset could be the reason she had displayed such detachment.

Hmm. Did she consider him in her niece's

younger age group and therefore too young for her? The thought piqued him. Did she not know she was a desirable woman, attractive to all men with eyes? That he was a man worthy of her?

He watched as woman and child studied Chloe's results of the rainbow chasing expedition, heads together. Chloe's hair was tied back in a rough ponytail and Isabel's features softened by glints of red amongst the free strands waving about her face like Aphrodite's.

His belly clenched with want, with the need to move on and open his heart to other women, to Isabel, and his brows drew together. There was no doubt he felt physical attraction to her. But was there any chance of reciprocation or just the spectre of more pain when she refused? She'd made no secret of the fact she wasn't interested in a dalliance.

Chloe skipped across and displayed her favourite frame to him and he dipped his head to study the screen. Indeed, the horizon sat straight and the composition did not look childish. It was a shot any amateur photographer could be proud of.

'A wonderful photograph of clouds and the rainbow.'

'Aunty Izzy taught me how to take pictures.'

He looked at Isabel. 'Your aunt is an excellent teacher.' Then back at the child. 'And you an excellent pupil. Your mother and papà will certainly enjoy this.' He listened to himself, stilted and awkward with the child. How had he fallen out of the way of talking to children? With people really.

This was good for him, this interaction. Rai would be pleased that he was, at least, trying.

'Can we send it now?' Chloe had spun to hold out the phone to her aunt.

'Now that we have the photo you want, let's go back to the house and have breakfast and dress properly for the day. We can send your surprise after breakfast, when Mummy has had a chance to wake up as well.'

'She won't be sleeping now.' Chloe looked askance at her aunt and Dom suppressed a smile. He doubted his brother would be sleeping either with his new wife in his bed.

Calmly, as she seemed to do everything, Isabel inclined her head. 'Just in case. Mummy has had a couple of very big days. It would be a shame to wake her if she were sleeping in.'

The child screwed her face until it cleared. 'After breakfast then. Can we ask Uncle Dom to breakfast?'

If he wasn't mistaken Isabel's face twitched before it returned to being expressionless. Dom felt the sudden unexpected mirth slip out from him in a small laugh. He put Isabel out of her misery. 'Thank you, little one, but I have already broken my fast.'

Isabel's expression did not change but he thought her shoulders loosened. Tiny nuances were there if he watched carefully. It seemed he liked watching carefully.

The child appeared determined to spend time with him. It gave him an unexpected warmth. But also forced his company on Isabel. He could see that wasn't her wish.

And why was that?

A devil inside him stirred. Yet he spoke to the child. 'We could meet for lunch, down at the beach kiosk.' Another twitch from her aunt and he suppressed his smile. 'I have not yet eaten there and would like to try it before I return to Italy.'

'Can we, Aunty Izzy? Lunch at the beach with Uncle Dom?'

'That's sounds delightful.' She smiled blandly and he inclined his head, a spurt of masculine pleasure shooting through him. He would give her delightful. Oh, yes.

A few hours later Dom read the email that confirmed with his secretary in Firenze that his flight would leave Australia on Christmas Eve. All the while he watched out of the window for Isabel.

The door of the house across the road opened and two females, one tall and one tiny, stepped along the path and out through the gate. Isabel did not glance his way but he noticed Chloe avidly searched for him, her gaze scanning the house from window to window. He huffed out a small laugh. His niece appreciated his company anyway.

He watched them turn to walk down the hill to the beach. Isabel was fifteen minutes early so he allowed them privacy to go ahead instead of rushing to join them for the walk, but still he closed his email and followed as soon as he could. He could see them ahead of him and took pleasure in watching Isabel sway sedately while his niece scampered ahead on the path.

His gaze returned to rest on Isabel, her dark auburn, sun-kissed hair tied back at her long, slender neck, head angled high, straight spine, this morning's long legs hidden by the swirl of a colourful ankle-length skirt. Isabel covered the ground gracefully like a dancer and he remembered again what it had been like to hold her in his arms at the wedding.

And the rehearsal before that.

She had been yielding and compliant, her breasts soft against his chest, her lovely body inherently balanced and responsive to his direction as the music slid over them both during the waltz. Yet it had not been enough. It had been in the dancing that his first moments of intrigue had turned to strong attraction, surprising him with unfamiliar longing after so long an abstinence.

When he'd come back into his brother's house this morning after the rainbow hunt, his anticipation for sharing lunch with Isabel and Chloe had also surprised him. He was eager. Though it was not a *date* as the Australians said. He doubted the self-sufficient woman would allow him to pay for her meal, even though it was his idea to go out, but that was a small battle he could win another time.

His chest felt lighter than it had for years as he closed the distance between them, noting in the periphery of his vision the rainbow of pastel cottages, colourful but paler than those in Cinque Terre or Burano yet still pretty.

The gardens were neat and colourful, and decorations abounded. The town seemed to smile and there was something healing about the sound of the sea as a constant gentle drumbeat in the distance.

The quiet path was a joy to travel on foot. Or was the joy in watching the child and woman ahead? His gaze lingered on Isabel and his heart lifted further.

The intrusive sound of motorbikes grew louder

in the distance and he decided this place felt too somnolent for young bloods, hotheads and speed. The engines of the bikes screamed closer, which didn't fit with the narrow streets and curving paths of the village, and he hoped the riders were as skilled at manoeuvring as they were at destroying the quiet.

The bikes and riders appeared like two red blurs, travelling far too fast, and he saw the moment Isabel reached the corner at the bottom and took the child's hand to pull Chloe to her.

The first bike braked, slowed and slewed to a stop at the unexpected T-intersection. Far too fast, the second bike tried, failed, slid out of control, tipped and spun sideways, the engine roar dropping as the rider tumbled off to bounce across the bitumen. The horizontal bike kept moving, shooting sparks in a roaring, grinding slide, the pings of flying gravel and the scream of metal scoring the road as it veered at alarming speed sideways towards Isabel and Chloe with unstoppable momentum.

Time slowed. Dom's vision sharpened and sounds rushed in. His breathing quickened, his mouth dried and his heart pounded with a sudden surge of energy. Dom began to run.

Isabel knew the bike would hit her but instinctively she swung her niece backwards towards the soft grass behind them where the little girl gasped at the unexpected shove, landed and rolled. Isabel felt the blow, the impact low and solid, taking her feet out from under her at the ankle, the rush of air as she was tossed through the air, but not by the bike.

By a man.

She'd been knocked aside from the machine by Dom, who landed on top of her, his big body covering hers as if to take the impact himself.

Her forehead hit the grass with a thwack and her body followed with a bone-jarring puff of breath exploding from her as weight crushed. The screech of metal and the crash of glass reverberated as the machine whooshed by with millimetres to spare and smashed into the telephone pole with a crumpling *whoomph*. The machine settled, tinkling a confetti of headlight glass and crumpling metal. Gradually the sounds died until only the sound of the sea and the *tink-tink* of a hot engine rose in the air. And the gallop of her heart.

The broken machine lay mere centimetres away, circling the pole like the palm of a tightening fist.

Chloe's frightened sob cleared Isabel's head of the shock from the impact and she tried to move.

'Chloe,' she gasped, struggling to pull air into

her squashed lungs while her ears rang from the bump to her head. 'Get off me.'

Dom shifted swiftly and with only a little stiffness, thankfully, she could breathe again.

Her heart pounded like a manic piston in her chest as he reached down to offer his hand and she took it, grateful for something solid to hang onto as everything else swam in her vision.

But thankful also, when she had time to think about it, for the fact he'd saved her from being mashed by the huge motorbike and hot metal against the unforgiving pole.

But Chloe first.

Isabel's ankle throbbed where she'd twisted to throw Chloe and then been hit by Dom. When she put her weight on her left foot, her lower leg screamed in protest and gave way. She would have fallen if he hadn't held her.

'Are you all right?' he asked.

'I think I've twisted something. And my head and shoulder hurt.'

He made a fast assessment of her face and body and lowered her again. 'I will bring Chloe to you. Then we will look closer.'

Seconds later he placed Chloe gently on the ground beside Isabel. Chloe's eyes were wide and confused and she reached for her aunt, who slid an arm around her.

Chloe stared into her face accusingly. 'You pushed me.'

Isabel dredged a smile from somewhere—goodness knew where it had been rummaged from—her heart still jolted and she couldn't stop thinking about how close to being hit she and Chloe had been. 'A good thing. I pushed you and Uncle Dom pushed me.' She pointed at the pole and wrecked vehicle. 'We didn't get squashed by the bike.'

And that was the gist of it.

Across the road the local policeman, still carrying the daily newspaper he'd just collected from the tiny newsagents, was gesticulating to the stationary motorcyclist and gesturing to Faith and Chloe on the footpath. Along with the hapless motorcyclist, who limped awkwardly, they all began to cross towards them.

Dom moved in front of Isabel and Chloe. To the men he said, *'Lo stupido.'* To the officer, in a cold rigid voice that, despite the lack of emotion, froze like dry ice, 'My family are both shaken. It is best we do not speak to these reckless people at this time.' He handed the policeman a card. 'My lawyers will be in contact with them.'

Isabel blinked. Lawyers? His card?

She said from the ground, tiredly, 'Nobody was hurt.'

Dom spun on her. 'You *are* hurt. Chloe is

bruised, I am sure. You both could have been dead.'

Yes, Chloe could have been killed. She shivered as cold slid over her skin in slivers of sick horror.

Then she saw the absolute terror in Domenico's eyes and with sudden insight wondered if he'd had a flashback to when he'd lost his own family. Not a lot of give in those eyes glaring back at her. He needed time-out more than she did. 'Take us home, please.'

He replied shortly. 'To the emergency department first, and then home.'

Dom said something else to the policeman, something low and gruff that she didn't hear, and the other men moved away towards the little police station across the street.

CHAPTER FOUR

WITHIN MINUTES OF Dom speaking to the policeman, a constable arrived in a police car to drive them across to the little hospital a few hundred metres away.

Dom carried her in, his strong arms holding her as if she were a precious porcelain doll, not a full-blooded woman capable of limping in herself, though if her head hadn't been swimming and her ankle aching so, she probably would have enjoyed the sensation of flying in Dom's arms.

Chloe followed with Isabel's handbag and a pinched worried frown on her little face. Poor Chloe.

What a mess this all was, Isabel thought, and wished they'd stayed home for lunch.

The emergency nurse ushered them to a stretcher in a cubicle and Dom made sure the staff knew he was a doctor and he wanted Isabel thoroughly examined. He asked for X-rays and an emergency doctor in a most demanding way.

'Sorry, Ro,' Isabel said quietly. As if they wouldn't get the best care. Despite her headache, she murmured, 'Domenico, let her do her job. Roseanne is very efficient.'

His attention shifted to her. 'You are hurt. I am partly responsible.'

Despite her awkwardness at his insistence to the nurse Isabel knew very well, there was a crazy, if illogical, delight in the fact he was so concerned about her. 'Thank you. But I'm good.'

Roseanne smiled at Isabel. 'He's fine. I can see he's worried.' She proceeded to assess Isabel's blood pressure and pulse. 'Normal.' And then checked her pupils. 'Both equal in size and briskly reacting to the light from my pencil torch,' she said as much for Dom as for Isabel. 'You've knocked your head. And we'll check your leg. Dr Southwell is coming.'

Isabel touched Dom's arm. 'Dr Southwell, Reg, is my friend Myra's husband.' *So be nice to him.* She didn't say it out loud, but his raised brows and slight smile said he got it.

'Ah,' he said, and glanced at his watch as if to say he should be here already.

The nurse smiled at Isabel. 'Lucky Reg is in the hospital.'

Isabel closed her eyes. 'So it seems.'

Reg arrived, rubbing the cleanser into his thin, age-spotted hands, his wrinkled face calm and kind. 'Isabel.' He looked at Dom.

Isabel said, 'You met Rai's brother, Dr Domenico Salvanelli, at the wedding. Dom, do you remember Dr Reg Southwell?'

The men nodded at each other and Reg turned back to her.

'Now, my dear. What have you been doing?' He took the chart from Roseanne and checked the observations then pulled on fresh gloves and crossed to her. Resting his fingers briefly on her wrist to feel her pulse, he said, 'I hear we had some less than intelligent motorcyclists causing problems.'

'Not for long,' Dom muttered.

There was a slight smile on Reg's face as he reached out and tilted her face so he could see the bumps and abrasions. He gently touched the place on her brow which was the worst of it and she winced. Dom stood at his shoulder watching and narrowed his eyes at her obvious discomfort. She wished he'd go outside and wait but she doubted anyone would be able to get him to leave. Again, a silly delight rose at the thought.

'Her ankle also is twisted. I hope not broken,' Dom said.

'We'll check that,' Reg said patiently. He moved

down to examine her leg. Glanced at Dom. 'What do you think?'

'I think badly sprained but not broken, but would prefer confirmation with an X-ray.'

Reg smiled. 'I agree.' He looked at Isabel. 'Are you happy for us to send you through to X-Ray? Perhaps Chloe's uncle could stay with her here, while you go through?'

By the time she returned, reassured by Reg, who'd come back when the X-rays had been processed and both he and Dom had discussed her leg bones ad nauseam, Isabel was allowed to go home in Dom's care.

The constable had waited and then driven them back up the hill to Isabel's house.

Once back at the top of the hill, Isabel tried to climb out of the vehicle under her own steam, despite the pain and the spinning in her head.

'Do not attempt to stand on that ankle.' Dom's growl came from behind her head and stopped her as she opened the front door of the patrol car. He was out of the back and at her side, his face grim and eyes flashing at her attempt at independence. Seemed she'd lost that one too.

'Why do you persist in foolishness?' he muttered and scooped her out and up as if she were lighter than Chloe. He stood, holding her, his arms securely pulling her against his big chest.

'Thank you,' he said to the policeman, dismissing him.

'Come, Chloe, perhaps you could find the keys to the door to your aunt's house in her handbag.' Chloe was still clutching it like a talisman through all the upheaval and drama of the morning.

Isabel shifted in his arms. 'I'm Chloe's great-aunt. Not her aunt.' As if reminding gave her some control. 'And the door is unlocked.'

He glared at her. 'Your foolish great-aunt.' And carried her into her house. He muttered a pithy comment about the fact the door was unlocked but Isabel ignored that particular point because it wasn't worth worrying over.

But his arms. They were a worry. Strong, so strong, yet tender, warm and very, very safe.

She couldn't remember the last time a man had carried her. Long back in childhood before her parents had passed. Never against such a broad, steel-banded chest, and seriously, that aftershave was to die for.

He placed her cautiously on her long sofa. As if she would break if he wasn't careful. 'We will pack and both you and Chloe will sleep across the road with me tonight.'

'No.'

He returned with two pillows from her room. 'Yes.' He placed them behind her then stood back and crossed his arms over that massive chest.

She raised her brows at him. Seriously? 'I'm not moving into Rai and Faith's house for the night.'

She needed an aspirin, or a paracetamol. Or a thimble of brandy. No. She couldn't have a brandy. Child-minding.

Memory sliced back to the accident.

She shivered. She and Chloe could have died. She'd pushed Chloe and Dom had saved her.

Still no reason to move in with him for twenty-four hours. Not happening. She wasn't losing this battle of wills.

Dom loomed over her as she sat with her legs up on the sofa.

'You need care. You must elevate the leg and should not walk. Walking on a sprained ankle is not advised.'

'I am aware of that. But it is only a sprain.'

He spoke impassively. 'Then you are aware that your ankle needs time to heal before weight-bearing. Twenty-four to forty-eight hours minimum. Weight-bearing too soon may slow healing or cause further damage. Then it could be a week of immobility.'

No, she didn't want that. 'I'm aware.'

'You are also possibly concussed and need cold compresses for your ankle.' Dom's face remained expressionless and hard, as if chiselled from the rock cliff-face down on the point of the bay. The one the waves beat against and never seemed to imprint.

He spread his fingers in that Mediterranean gesture so many Italian men seemed to love. 'How is your five-year-old niece going to look after you?'

She'd manage. In private. No big dark Italian to watch her struggle. 'We'll be fine.'

His lips compressed in a firm tight line, but his expression said he doubted that very much. She wondered if eyebrows could be arrogant as she watched his rise with exasperation up into his dark hairline.

She closed her eyes, feeling light-headed and silly with shock, and said in a small voice, 'If you'd like to do something I can't ask of Chloe…' She flicked open her lashes and re-assured herself Chloe was still fine. Her niece looked none the worse for the morning's excite-ment, playing with her dolls as she explained about motorbikes and being careful on roads to her plastic friends. 'I would very much like a cup of black tea with some sugar or honey, please.'

Dom made an odd snorting, infuriated noise, but turned away for the kitchen. She'd missed the opportunity to see what the noise had meant.

She closed her eyelids again and rested back on the heaped pillows he had scooped from her bed.

Scooped from her bed.

He'd seen her bedroom.

That left her with an odd, tingling feeling she was so not going to examine.

It seemed like seconds later but must have been minutes because the kitchen electric jug had been cold and her tea steamed beside her with wafts of sweet honey scent. Dom knelt beside her leg to examine her ankle without touching. Waiting for her to open her eyes.

'You slept.'

'I did not.' Had she?

Dom didn't bother arguing. In his hand lay two round white pills. Paracetamol, she recognised. She took them and sipped from the glass of water beside the tea.

'We will hold off on the ibuprofen until your headache is gone, in case of concussion. Later you may start them for the swelling of your leg. But I have ice for your ankle.'

He crouched down beside her and that wondrous, masculine Dom scent wafted over her. Clean and spicy and too darn yummy. 'May I check again that it is not showing signs of more than a simple sprain?'

He'd already had her checked, he'd checked

her, along with Chloe, and everyone had been satisfied that there were no broken bones.

It did hurt like the blazes, though. 'Fine. And thank you for the ice.' Manners. She needed to watch those manners, which seemed to go haywire in his presence. 'And the tea. And tablets. It was very kind of you.'

There. She sounded more like herself again.

He glanced up at her. Smiled. As if he'd heard her thoughts.

'It must be very tender.' His long fingers slid along the red swelling on the outside of her calf, carefully probing. The slight pressure made her wince. And his touch made her warm. All over. He'd removed her shoes as soon as he'd put her down, so the polish on her toes winked like little red eyes when she shifted her feet. For some weird reason she found that embarrassing.

Her ankle would be fine. There was no odd shaping despite the raised bump, but the whole lower leg had turned red and swollen.

He straightened and stood. 'Ankle tendons are strong, but sudden overstretching and strain—' here a brief shrug '—such as caused by a large man knocking you sideways can cause damage.' He dipped his head. 'My apologies.'

Her cheeks felt hot. Too much large man too close. 'I forgive you for saving my life,' she said lightly, but she was feeling anything but light with Dom's hands so recently on her ankle. It was as if the heat was still there. And creeping higher.

He smiled and the warmth of that curve of his lips did something inside her she couldn't control. An unfurling and wanting she couldn't think about. Unfair. Too beautiful and caring for a man she barely knew and had banned herself from giving false hope to. Banned from giving herself false hope.

He turned his big body sideways and took the bag of ice he must have made up from her freezer trays and wrapped in one of her tea towels. He lowered the pack slowly and gently on top of her lower leg and sat back.

Then he handed her the cup of tea and made sure she could reach the table to put it down again.

'You should come to Raimondo's house for the night,' he tried again.

'No.'

Dom sighed, perhaps with some long-suffering edge to it, and glanced instead around the room. His gaze settled on the large soft white leather reclining armchair she'd bought last week, a little luxury she planned to curl up in and read her book now that she was the single occupant of the house. The seat swivelled all ways and towards the windows looking out to

the small ocean-facing veranda. 'Then I will
stay here. I will use that chair.'

'What do you mean, stay?' She'd turned
Faith's room into an office. There was only
Chloe's single bed. And hers.

'Once I have returned with my laptop and
phone charger I will visit with you and Chloe
today. I will come and go. Tonight, I will sleep—'
he pointed one long finger imperiously '—there.'

'No, you won't.'

He didn't argue that either, but she knew darn
well that didn't mean he'd agreed to sleep in
his own bed across the road. The worst of it
was, she probably needed him. And that only
made her more uncomfortable. She didn't want
to need anyone because when she had trusted a
man to be there for her before he'd abandoned
her.

Her head ached and her leg throbbed. She
would deal with this other—larger—irritation
later.

'You need to rest. Avoid activities that cause
pain, swelling or discomfort. That means walking. We will use the ice pack for fifteen to
twenty minutes and repeat every two to three
hours while you are awake. But I will check
every hour if I am not already here.'

All sensible advice. She didn't argue.

He frowned down at her. 'I will set my phone

alarm and ensure that we follow this timing. But first, compression. I wish to reinforce the flimsy bandage they have applied, to help stop the swelling.' He held up a wide bandage she suspected he'd found in her first aid box.

Hourly checks, alarms? The man was pedantic.

And how had he discovered her emergency medical supplies?

As if hearing her aunt's thoughts, Chloe appeared at her side. 'I showed Uncle Dom where to find the bandages.'

Oh. 'Thank you, Chloe. That was very helpful.'

Chloe's worried little face relaxed, as if she'd been unsure if she'd done the right thing. She handed Isabel a small packet of hand freshener wipes. 'You have dirt on your face.'

Poor little mite. Such drama and strangeness to face when her mummy had just gone away. 'What a clever girl you are.' She took the wipes and cleaned her hands and face. 'Does that look better?'

Chloe nodded and smiled. 'And my dolls and I showed Uncle Dom where the bags are to put the ice in. And the tea towels for wrapping.' Now she looked mighty pleased with herself.

'You and your dolls are such wonderful people to have around when I have a sore ankle. And you are playing so well.'

Chloe would be fine with just the two of them. She was an independent little girl with a sunny nature and biddable disposition. Which Isabel believed came from the absolute knowledge that everyone loved her and that she was a big help to her mother and aunt. Discipline had always been loving and gentle and the rewards were in front of her.

'Do you know how to use your aunt's phone, Chloe?' Dom's voice startled Isabel out of her rambling thoughts. Her phone, she saw now, had appeared on the table beside her. When had that happened? Another thing he'd asked Chloe for?

'Yes,' Chloe said, instantly bright-eyed and eager.

Dom picked it up. Swiped and looked satisfied it wasn't automatically locked. Proceeded to add a number to the contacts.

He could have asked first. 'Lucky I haven't a photo of myself in a bikini as a screenshot.'

'Or bad luck,' Dom said with a straight face.

Just like a man. She deserved that. She held back a smile at the thought.

'You can press this number—' he showed Chloe the screen '—and I will answer, if you or your aunt need my help when I am not here.'

In between those hourly visits? Isabel felt her

cheeks heat. Did he think she couldn't survive between his welfare checks? Good grief. 'She won't have to do that,' she said.

'Perhaps not. But if she does need me... Would you prefer she cross the road to my brother's house without a chaperone?' He tilted his head as if speaking to someone whose sense had deserted them. 'This is better.'

Isabel's hands tightened in her lap. No Mediterranean gestures for her, but she wanted to throw them out in a 'Good grief' gesture like he had. And, worse, she knew the darn man was right. She had fallen asleep just minutes ago.

Discreetly she blew an easing sigh and let the tension go. 'Of course. Thank you.' Her voice sounded sweet. Maybe a bit too sweet but that was the best she could manage. Her usual common sense and desire for independence felt torn and shredded, as if it had deserted her where this man was involved. And her head ached. She needed to go to the bathroom and wondered if she could hop across while Dom was gone. But she suspected it would be fraught with the weakness she still felt.

'Rest your eyes, *cara*. I will return soon.'

CHAPTER FIVE

DOM SHUT HIS MOUTH. Felt his face harden in shock. *Cara?* His Teresa had been *cara*, not this woman he'd met just over a week ago.

He put down Isabel's phone and turned to the door. 'I will be back in twenty minutes to remove the ice.' He ignored Isabel's 'Chloe can do that,' called after him and strode out.

His mind whirled. His chest thumped. His skin itched. It had been an unconscious use of the endearment. Just a slip of the tongue. Concern for a woman in distress and an unintended softening.

It meant nothing.

Or did it mean he was changing? Opening his heart to Chloe's Aunty Izzy, calling her *cara*, the first time the word had passed his lips since that dark day of his loss? Or was it only delayed shock from the events of the morning and not his heart at all?

Cara Isabel?

Faith's rock when Rai had failed her.

Dom's damsel in distress whom he'd injured in saving.

Isabel's presence had shoved him by the shoulder that first day until his senses opened and he saw her. Saw her calm, her empathy and her ability to manage the unexpected. Saw her humour directed at him, understated but skimming the surface in the glances he caught from her. She would make someone a good wife. The thought furrowed his brow at the thought of another man with Isabel. Or she could make him a good wife.

Why was he thinking this? He did not love her like he'd loved his Teresa, but...

The way she managed Chloe—managed everything and everyone—made him consider the thought with more calm. Less emotion.

Suddenly it seemed he did miss not having a partner in life. A wife to lie down with at night. To wake up to with the sun. To share his thoughts and his body and his soul. In fact, in the awareness between him and Isabel, something powerful could grow if only she would help him nurture it.

This new wanting of her was making him a little crazy.

Isabel Fetherstone had been hurt but could she really be cast as a woman in distress when she was so capable, so steady, so sensible? Isabel's distress came from having to rely on him, not from the fact that he had wrenched her ankle and forced her head to the ground.

She'd saved his niece. She had thought very quickly to ensure Chloe's safety and not her own. She could have been crushed against the pole by the metal monster. But she hadn't been. He'd saved her. He'd saved Isabel.

At that thought his mind cleared and the tension in his shoulders eased somewhat. He needed to apprise his brother of what had happened, but he'd wait for Isabel and Chloe to be present before making the call.

Their planned time for lunch had passed and no doubt Chloe would also be hungry. So much for his booking a table at the café. Perhaps the establishment would do takeaway in the circumstances and deliver.

He pulled out his phone as he crossed the street to his brother's house and pressed the café's number.

Twenty minutes later Dom knocked and pushed open the door to Isabel's cottage. He carried a small overnight satchel with toiletries, his computer and chargers. Soon a large box of food would be delivered here.

Strange how the idea that he was compelled

to attend to an invalid, and to a night's sleep on a chair, did not bother him.

'You're back.' Isabel's demeanour appeared less shaken, the tea and water had been consumed, and a light blush of colour had returned to her cheeks. She looked rested. Unruffled. Breathtaking.

He cleared his throat and stamped down his sudden urge to cross the room and sit by her. 'I have ordered for lunch to be delivered.'

She smiled, her face alight with a touch of mischief, an appreciation of his actions and a cordiality that was growing between them. His chest warmed. Such a smile was worthy of more than a box of food. She gestured towards the back of the cottage. 'Chloe is playing with her dolls in her room.'

Good. This meant the child was over the shock of the accident. And gave him a chance to be alone with Isabel?

'I have come to remove the ice.' He put his overnight bag down beside the chair and moved across to lift the soggy towel of ice from her ankle. He carried it across to the sink, then returned to crouch beside her.

'Let me look.' The skin above and below the bandage where the ice had lain was pale with cold but not swollen. He slid his finger carefully on the uninjured side to feel the tightness between her skin and the bandage. 'Firm but not too tight.'

He glanced up at her face. Her eyes twinkled at him though her expression remained composed.

'Everything is good. You have an excellent bedside manner,' she added.

Was she teasing him? But she seemed serene and sincere. So he answered honestly. 'A bedside manner is not something I practice often.'

'You are a doctor, yes?'

He was not a doctor. Not any more. Though lately he had thought… 'Apart from some crisis relief with my brother in Third World countries, and occasional relief in one of the poorer villages for a friend of mine, I have mostly been a pharmacist for many years.' One of the brothers had had to promise their grandfather they would carry on the company. With his wife and son dead, Dom hadn't cared about anything. It hadn't mattered. Nothing had mattered. No. He had not been a doctor for years.

'You still have medical skills. Look at your care for my ankle. It feels better already.' She cast him a quick hopeful look. 'In fact, it feels so much better you really don't need to stay.'

Ha. He understood her tactic. 'But I do. I shall plan to stay tonight.' He shrugged. 'Tomorrow we will see how independent you are.'

He thought her lips might have compressed and wasn't sure why that amused him. Her eyes did not meet his. Deliberately? To hide her expression?

They both stared down at her leg. It was a very nice leg.

He asked softly, 'And your headache?'

Unconsciously she lifted her hand to her forehead, where a small bruise blossomed beneath the graze that marked her brow. 'Better.'

He wondered how 'better' it really was and would have liked to smooth it. But her defences were up, he could tell. 'May I check the reactions of your pupils again?'

'Of course.' Her head lifted and he saw how such a request gave tension to her shoulders. Was this because it brought him closer? He hoped so. Because when he was close he could breathe her floral scent and admire the sheen of her skin. And he liked the way she blushed.

He took her chin in his hand and shone the torch. Once he was satisfied that both pupils were equal in size and reacting to the light from his small torch, he stood.

Before awkwardness could descend on their silence, a knock sounded at the front door.

He felt movement at his side as he crossed the room and when he opened it Chloe was peering out with him. It was the food.

He'd ordered for ease of consumption. Chicken and salad wraps for everyone, Pizza Margherita to share and a bowl of finger-sized whiting fillets with chips. For dessert, small pots of ice-cream and berries. A takeaway cappuccino for Isabel, cola for him and a milkshake for Chloe.

Anything that wasn't eaten he could leave in Isabel's refrigerator for her convenience later.

Her gaze was on him as he crossed the room and she said, 'I've been waiting to call Faith and Rai.'

He put the box on the round table she used for meals. 'I thought also but waited for you. You look well enough to do this now. And that we both agree they should be told and reassured.'

Isabel nodded. 'I thought Chloe could phone them. That way, Faith will know she's fine right from the beginning and then we can both reassure them.'

So they did. On speaker phone—not something he was fond of.

Chloe's explanation startled him. 'Mummy, it's Chloe. I'm on Aunty Izzy's phone and a motorbike crashed. Aunty Izzy tossed me onto the grass, so I'm fine. Uncle Dom's not so good at tossing Aunty Izzy. Now she has a sore leg and a headache.'

Dom froze, horrified, and then he bit his lip to stop his smile, turning his head to Isabel, who held her hand over her mouth. Her eyes danced like green gems in the light and their gazes met and connected. He had forgotten the joy of a child's viewpoint and sharing it with Isabel was even more delightful.

A sizzle of awareness zinged between them, pausing his breath. It seemed he had also forgotten the strength of a visual connection across a room from a woman he desired.

On the phone speaker, Faith's exclamations of horror came with an instant offer to return home.

'May I talk to Mummy, please, Chloe?' Isabel accepted the phone from her niece. 'You're not coming home because of this. You'll be back the day after tomorrow and I'm feeling much better already.'

Dom held back impatience but as words continued between them—a back-and-forth negotiation that was going nowhere—he held up his hand. This could be long and drawn out in the way of women. 'I wish to speak to Raimondo, please.'

Isabel narrowed her eyes at him. Dom blinked as she frowned. Such an expression! She was holding his gaze with what looked like censure.

What? he wondered and closed his mouth. He thought about her frown as he waited and replayed his request in his mind. Or had it been an order? In six years had he grown out of practice in dealing with those who did not work for him?

'Domenico wishes to speak to Rai,' she was telling Faith. Her voice held a trace of astringency. 'Chloe and I are both fine. We just felt we needed to make you aware of our adventure.'

He should have called his brother on his own phone. That would have been a simple solution without machinations. He held up his hand.

She paused again, still annoyed. The slight frown was unaccustomed censure from this woman. She said, 'Just a minute,' to Faith.

'I will phone Raimondo myself. You are not to be rushed in talking to Faith.' He inclined his head, acknowledging that he had been abrupt. 'My apologies.'

Isabel lifted her gaze and her face softened. She nodded. 'Dom said he would call Rai himself. Yes, I will tell you what happened in more detail now the men are sorted but everything is fine. Honestly.'

Dom heard the shortening of his name and hid his pleased smile. She had referred to him as Dom. The first of many barriers he wanted gone. Perhaps the start of her letting him in. They had been through fraught circumstances of course, but still…a good sign. He opened the front door and pressed the number for his brother.

* * *

Isabel watched Dom leave the open-plan house to step back into the front courtyard. Two mobile phone conversations would have been annoying, so it was good he was gone. That didn't stop her from wishing she could hear his side of the conversation with Rai.

'Tell me again?' Faith's voice recalled her to the phone in her hand.

She explained again in more detail and after five more minutes, and another quick conversation with Chloe, Faith sounded satisfied that all was well and the call ended. Isabel had played down her sore ankle which, although feeling better after the ice and the pain medication, she knew would be a nuisance.

Dom had still not returned and Chloe drifted to the box of wrapped food and aromas filling the room with a woebegone look on her face. 'Can we have lunch now?'

'As soon as Uncle Dom is back. He's talking to your papà.'

'What if he takes hours?'

'That would be a problem.' She looked at the little girl. Chloe needed her lunch and was still tired from her recent illness. She needed a sleep after such an exciting morning. 'I'll text him.'

She found the number and did it quickly, before she chickened out.

Chloe is starving. Would you mind if we start without you?

Twenty seconds later Dom returned, smiling. He looked ten years younger when he did so and the smile was so rare to see it took her breath away. Though the seven years younger thing was a worry. She was feeling particularly old just at this moment.

'Thank you for reminding me of the lunch,' he said as he closed the door behind him. 'Of course Chloe must eat. The food will grow cold.'

He moved to the table but Chloe tugged on his trouser leg. 'Uncle Dom. We have to wash our hands before we touch food.'

Isabel sucked in her breath and winced. She'd need to prompt Chloe gently not to boss adults.

Dom's head lifted and, to her relief, she saw the effort he made not to laugh. 'Thank you, Chloe.' He crouched and looked at his niece. 'That is true. Thank you. It has been such a busy morning I am forgetting things.'

Chloe nodded approval and showed the way to the sink and proceeded to wash her own hands. 'That's okay. Aunty Izzy always says I am a good girl when I remember.'

They shared the soap and the water and Chloe offered her hand towel to dry. 'This is my special towel. Aunty Izzy sewed a lighthouse on it for me. You can use it.'

Dom looked across at her and she shrugged. Yes, she could sew. He looked back at the child. 'Thank you, Chloe.' His big hands were too large for the small scrap of material.

Then they attacked the box of goodies. Isabel wiped her fingers again with one of Chloe's little wipes and tried not to laugh as Chloe directed Dom on which things to serve her.

They ate off plastic plates because that was the cupboard Chloe could reach and Dom filled Isabel's plate with small portions of everything. The coffee when sipped had stayed hot enough and Isabel closed her eyes as she drank. Bliss. Perhaps her headache hadn't been helped by missing her coffee. She'd somehow omitted this morning's caffeine. The time for their planned lunch was well past now and she needed it.

Dom sat across from her, consuming his food economically with little attention, but paying attention to Isabel's needs, while she encouraged Chloe to finish so she could have a rest. When Chloe had finally eaten what she wanted she drooped as she sat, and Isabel shifted to rise.

'No.' Dom gestured. 'Stay.'

No? Stay? She was tempted to reply with a 'Woof'. Funny how she was lying down for these orders she'd normally rail against. Her head must be woozy.

'May I tuck you in, Chloe? That way, Aunty Izzy can keep her leg up.'

Minutes later Dom came back from Chloe's room smiling the new amused smile that Chloe seemed to drag out of him. It looked good on him. 'She is a quaint child with a kind heart.'

Isabel reran those words through her mind. Quaint? Kind? Such old-fashioned words. But true, yes. Chloe was both of those things and it pleased her that Dom could see these admirable qualities in his niece. 'She likes you.'

His eyes rolled at that. As if it wasn't true. Of course she liked her big handsome uncle. The man had issues.

'Through no effort of mine, I believe. I look like her new papà, that is all.' He shrugged those massive shoulders and, despite her attempt not to, her gaze followed the stretch of the fabric as he shifted. Such an impressive build and yet not too heavy. She marvelled that she hadn't heard the creak of tortured fabric. Remembered she was staring and pulled her eyes away.

Funny how she noticed Dom's broadness. While many men were built with strength and size, she wasn't drawn to smooth their skin or want to bury her face in their chests. Just his. Dom's. Every angle she had of Dom—and at the moment he soared above her—looked delightfully attractive to her.

Isabel murmured, 'You don't look exactly the same as your brother.'

He repeated the shrug and again she enjoyed the show. Straight-faced, he said, 'I am the more handsome, of course.'

Isabel blinked and returned her gaze to his face. He did not just say that, did he? Then she got it. 'You made a joke?'

His brows went up. 'Have I been such a sorry soul this shocks you?'

'Shock?' she murmured. Then shut her mouth. It might have been shock. Certainly surprise. 'No. Of course not,' she continued calmly. Settled herself after all the silly emotions that seemed to be floating and spinning in her addled brain. 'I'm pleasantly relieved, Domenico.' Her own joke.

He smiled. 'Come. You have called me Dom once. You can do so again. From now on, I hope.'

It shouldn't have been so hard to say his name out loud. 'Dom.' She said it a little too forcefully and darned if her cheeks didn't grow warm with heat.

He smiled. Getting a lot of those, she thought. Seemed a girl needed to be almost killed to start him smiling.

'How is your headache?' he asked, his expression growing serious with concern again.

She couldn't have that and smiled airily. 'Almost gone. The coffee helped, so thank you for bringing me that much-needed caffeine.'

'You are most welcome.'

The conversation had run its course and silence fell between them. This time the emptiness filled with tension and awareness. Their eyes met and held. Enough. She needed space. Air to breathe because he was stealing it from her lungs. She had to try again to make him leave. To get some space to regain her senses, which were now topsy-turvy from more than the effects of the accident.

'As I said, there really is no need for you to stay with us here when you have things to do. You've barely seen anything of the bay and you're leaving soon. We both know how to contact you if we're desperate.'

'And yet I will stay.' An expressionless man, no longer smiling. 'Would you be more comfortable on your bed for a rest while Chloe is asleep? I will sit out here in case she wakes. You could give the last of your headache the chance to disappear if you slept.'

It was a good idea. But she suspected Dom would feel the need to carry her into her room and the idea made her squirm with tension, and heat and want. She wasn't supposed to want those things. Not if she wasn't going to encourage him.

She remembered the last time his arms had held her. Safety and strength and scent.

Could imagine it again. Far too easily. But the bathroom would be good.

'You think too much,' he said quietly and stood, all man and all ready to take command. 'We both know it is a good idea. Are you stubborn, Isabel?'

She suspected she was acting that way. Sighed in defeat. 'If you give me your arm I would like to go to the bathroom.'

He leaned forward. 'I will give you both of my arms.' He said it simply and just as simply he picked her up and carried her through to the bathroom, stood her on one leg beside the sink and ensured she had a firm grip. 'Are you steady and balanced?'

'Yes. Thank you.' Primly.

She was relieved he left without looking back. No man had ever taken her to the ladies. Good grief.

Isabel stared in the mirror as the door shut. She had a graze on her cheek, but even the one not grazed looked pink from embarrassment. Blushing, at her age. The bump on her forehead looked purple. She grimaced.

Grow up, Aunt Isabel. Think of him as a male nurse. That made her chew her lip with amusement.

Then urgency reminded her she was here for a reason.

Once she'd finished in the bathroom, washed her hands and cleaned her teeth, Isabel knew she couldn't stand much longer without falling over. Her ankle had developed a throbbing pulse of pain with every heartbeat and the ache grew more insistent the longer she hung it down. She hopped to the door of the bathroom and opened it, looking for her nurse.

Dom rose from the white chair and crossed to her. He studied her face, which she'd noticed in the mirror had paled, and bent towards her. 'Your bed, I think.'

His arms and hands and fingers came around her again. Big, warm, safe. BWS. Like the initials of an Australian liquor store chain and just as addictive as its wares.

He reminded her of one of those dark, silky chocolate whisky liquors. A heady mix. Intoxicating and smooth as it burned and warmed and slid all the way down her throat. Like heat down her body. Like hot fingers on her skin.

Whoa there. No fingers were sliding anywhere. She was going down on the bed to rest.

He'd slowed. Stopped walking. Stood before her door and looked down into her face, untroubled by her tall frame in his arms, as relaxed as if she weighed no more than Chloe.

'What?' Caught by something he saw in her face. 'Are you daring me to kiss you, Isabel?'

Good grief. Had he read her thoughts? She hoped not. 'I've always thought dares were silly.'

'And what if I dare you to kiss me?'

'I am not so foolish.' But Isabel's body had melted to soft and languorous with her thoughts.

'Scared?' His dark eyes crinkled wickedly. His face drew closer.

'No. Not scared.' Her gaze dropped from those all-seeing eyes to his mouth. Full, curved lips. Sexy lips. Sinful lips. The impulsive Isabel of old would have tilted her face and pulled his head down to hers. She wanted to.

His voice caressed as his lips parted. 'Prove it.'

A dare the old Isabel would have taken.

And the new Isabel?

Isabel leaned up and he leaned down. Their lips brushed. Tingled. Supped in sliding, seductive sideways nibbles. A tide of longing surged between them, tossing her intentions of a fast peck aside and forcing her mouth more firmly against his. Her fingers tangled with the silky strands of his hair and her lips parted. She opened to his hot and honeyed mouth and heat blasted. Scorching and terrifying.

She froze, wiped the expression from her face and eased away.

'Do not stop,' he whispered. 'Come back.'

'I choose not to.' She battled not to flush with her thoughts.

She tried not to hurry into speech but the words came out too fast. 'Put me down, Dom.'

She needed to be out of his arms. Before she threw her own around him. 'We're grateful you were here when all this happened. Thank you for pushing me out of the way, Domenico.'

'Dom. And we know I added a little to your injuries.' Words tumbling as if to hide the kiss.

She mumbled, 'It could have been so much worse if the bike had picked me up in passing and squashed me against the pole.'

And that was true. She had been lucky. The thought of that—and getting that worst-case scenario out of her mind and into words—strangely settled her. As if there were worse things than enjoying being in the arms of a handsome man. Kissing Dom.

His fingers tightened their hold until they gripped her a little too firmly, as if affected by her words. 'I do not like to think of that possibility.' He looked into her face, his strong features so close to her own. 'The thought of you being hurt pains me.'

Don't kiss me again. She hid her thoughts beneath her eyelids.

'Would have pained me too. Thank you.' Trying to lighten the mood, she attempted a smile but it wobbled around the edges. His hold eased as if he realised he was clutching her too tight.

'You are most welcome.' He tilted his head as if struck, and his eyes widened as if he'd just noticed her agitation. 'Now you are nervous in my arms. From one kiss?' A slow, teasing smile tilted his lips that were again too close to hers. He began to walk again. 'No need for that. We will play more dares another day.'

Oh, my. Another day. Isabel tried to disperse some of the response from her body but tension pulled her tight. Heating her belly. Tickling her skin with awareness. She wanted to say she wasn't nervous. Of now or the future. Liar. After that kiss, something was going on with her responses that she couldn't shut down.

'Not nervous,' she blurted but her cheeks burned and she tried to look away to hide her lying eyes. Dom held her captured in the depth of his scrutiny. Delving into her thoughts, as if seeing something he'd missed before.

His brows drew together. Then his eyes widened. 'And not the truth.' He laughed. 'Isabel, dissembling is not your forte. A woman who cannot lie. There is fun to be had with you in this.'

Oh, great, she thought, and was pretty sure her ears were burning too with embarrassment.

'But not while you are injured,' he clarified thoughtfully while his mouth tilted more. 'For now, it is time for you to rest.'

And what the heck did that mean? Did he have plans to carry her around and tease her another day? Play truth and dare with her? Did Italians even know that game? She turned her face away so he couldn't see her expression, but she felt flushed and embarrassed and after that possibly too stimulated for sleep.

As he lowered her she saw that while she'd been in the bathroom he'd brought the pillows back from the sofa. Plumped up and soft, he'd put two pillows at the head of the bed, and one positioned lengthways for her leg.

Inside, her chest tightened. She had always been the one to pick up after others. Be the support in crisis, yet always in the background. The one who put other's needs before her own. Even in her very few relationships, no man had done little comfort things for her like this.

Dom had even found the soft blanket on the chair that she kept for cool evenings. The space he'd created on her bedcovers looked inviting and he leaned over and placed her gently in the centre of the quilt like a fragile flower.

Then in one movement and with experienced hands he floated the fluffy throw over her until warmth settled feather-light around her. As if she were a child. Or precious. The softness against her skin settled some of the emptiness she felt at his release.

'Thank you.' Still feeling oddly small in the middle of the mattress with him looming over her.

He stepped back, as if he read her reaction. 'Rest.'

He left her staring at the ceiling.

He needed an heir. He wasn't for her. But, for the moment, it felt secretly special to be the recipient of such care. And despite the thoughts chasing and the sensations still thrilling in her ribcage she was able to close her eyes. Another amazing thought was that she could trust him to keep Chloe safe if she fell asleep, and that was good.

Three hours later Dom woke Isabel with tea. It was time to add ice to her leg anyway. He'd placed his own cup beside the window chair in her room and gone back for hers, hoping she would wake with the coming and going, but she hadn't.

It concerned him that she should sleep so heavily after a knock on the head. And a kiss that had shaken them both.

He'd been anxious for an hour now and had slipped in to count her heartrate twice to check she was medically stable. Her delicate wrist had pulsed slow and steady and she'd murmured once in sleep, turning her face to him with a soft smile. Definitely not awake, because she did not look at him with that gentle pleasure when conscious.

He wanted her to feel pleasure when she looked at him. The way he did when he looked at her. He remembered her mouth on his and wanted it again. But kissing in a dare did not really count. He wanted her to see him as a man with desire for her. Possibly—some time in the future—even *her* man, not just a young male relative by marriage she'd had to rely on.

At this moment she looked so peaceful and he resisted the urge to stroke her cheek with his finger. Concerned he would startle her, now he placed the cup on her bedside table with a small clunk and she stirred and opened her eyes.

'*Buonasera*, Isabel,' he said, and leant forward to offer his hand to help her sit up. 'Chloe is awake and colouring in her book quite happily.'

'I slept,' she said, and he smiled.

'Indeed. It is four p.m. and I thought you would not sleep tonight if I let you sleep much longer.'

Her eyes widened at the passage of time. 'Good grief.'

It was her favourite saying, he decided, pleased to have this one personal insight. 'How is your headache?' he asked.

She closed her eyes and opened them again. He saw the pupils contract and nodded. Then he was so distracted by the emerald pools he couldn't help staring into them until she looked away.

'Headache is fading,' she murmured.

The bruise was not. The mark on her forehead seemed a deeper purple than before.

He retreated to the chair beside the bed and sat down. Yes, he was being unfair, standing over her in her room. 'I hope you don't mind. I brought my own tea to share while you have yours.'

'Of course.' She looked through the door to where he knew she could see Chloe. 'Thank you. I could get used to you bringing me tea in bed. Though I'm a coffee girl in the mornings.' She put her hand up. 'I'm joking, of course.'

She blushed for some reason and it was so delightful he'd have liked to discuss the concept of him being here in the mornings. Tease her. Watch her blush more. But she was hurrying on. 'It seems I did need your welfare check if I slept through Chloe waking. I know what a little chatterbox she is after a nap.'

'Sleep is a good healer.' Though he had never found it so. He touched his own head to explain. 'You need ice on your bruise as well. After you finish your tea, we will see to that.'

The rest of the day was more of the same, Dom trying to anticipate Isabel's needs, Chloe ridiculously happy to have them both close and attentive. Isabel, it seemed, was too sore to care that she had lost her independence for the moment. The doctor in him watched her carefully for complications. The man fell more under her spell each hour that he spent with her. She was like the princess in the fairy tale he had never believed in. He still wasn't sure that he did believe.

CHAPTER SIX

ISABEL WAS WOKEN the next morning by a phone call from Faith to say they were coming home a day early.

'I'm disappointed,' Isabel said out loud when she'd completed the call.

Dom stood at the door of her room with a cup in his hand, an enquiring look on his aristocratic face. The man looked like a Renaissance hero; she could imagine him reaching down to pull her onto his horse, hard thighs against hers, his chest a wall behind her, one arm around her to ride away...

Good grief. Thankfully the aroma of coffee swirled into the room on a drift of air and dispelled the dream.

She wanted coffee. And him. But she could only have the first one.

'You are disappointed in my *caffè*?'

What? Oh. She'd said 'disappointed'. She had to laugh. 'No. Coffee smells wonderful, thank you. I'm disappointed in Faith and Rai coming home early.'

He stepped closer and placed the aromatic cup beside her on the night table then leaned and took the pillow from the quilt, tucking it behind her head and helping her to sit up. As if she were a weightless leaf from a tree rather than a full-grown woman.

Morning assistance from her magnificent nurse.

Then she remembered Faith. 'They're coming home today. Have already left.' She huffed. 'Their brief honeymoon was already too short!'

'They have a life together now.' Dom didn't seem fazed but then he would be free of responsibility once Chloe returned to her parents. 'And if you had been in your niece's place? Would you have stayed away?'

Darn it. No. She would have been back last night.

That realisation made her cross and she never got cross. Well, not often before Dom swashbuckled into her life.

She looked at the tall man watching her face with amusement. Amusement was good on him and she squashed the spurt of irritation in herself. He'd brought her coffee. Had slept in a chair between his self-imposed three-hourly attentions. She owed him thanks and serenity and a modicum of good humour.

What was it about this man who made it so hard to stay settled in her quiet life, content with her few friends, ecstatic with her privacy and the solitude of her new home? Dom's arrival and intrusion into her life had affected her ability to remain even-tempered and she didn't know how to stop that snowball of emotion rolling down the hill all the way to the beach below.

But she'd have to stop it. Build a wall again. Think normal thoughts.

She sipped her coffee slowly—it was so good, just right. She rarely managed to make it so delicious even though she'd owned the machine for years.

Dom sat opposite and drank his own small cup in the chair by the window.

Apparently he'd claimed that chair for himself.

She suspected it wouldn't look right now without him in it.

Once she'd drained her cup she slid back the covers and lifted her damaged leg across and out. Pain pulled, better but still there, and she hissed her attempt to hold it in.

'Do you need the bathroom?'

'No.' Her eyes narrowed at him. 'I need my independence.'

He shrugged, refusing to respond to her ill humour. 'Which you cannot have until your ankle has recovered.' He tilted his head at her. 'I did not think you would be a difficult patient, Isabel, but I see I was mistaken.'

She huffed out a laugh. 'I'm trying, and you're right, not always successfully. And if you were in my place,' she muttered, referencing his previous comment about Faith coming home.

He laughed. It was short and awkward, as if he were out of practice and he'd surprised himself. He'd sure as heck surprised her.

'Of course, yes, I would be the same. So perhaps I do sympathise with your frustration. I will send in your niece, who has been waiting for you to wake up, and she will be delighted to find your clothes for you. Then I will help you to the bathroom.'

By the look in his eyes she could tell he'd decided to carry her.

She could fight it—should fight it—she was being weak, turning herself into a wimp wanting to be coddled. But you know what? He'd be gone soon. Why the heck would any sane woman refuse Dom in all his glory?

Because it was bad for her.

Like eating a whole box of chocolates at once.

Sweet Dom. Strangely, she found her good humour restored.

'It is almost time for the ice again,' Dom said with a check of his watch.

Isabel sought her usual Zen state of calm and sense. When the twenty-four hours had passed, they could stop the ice. Three hourly cold compresses for twenty minutes each through the night, attended to by Dom, and one trip to the bathroom being carried. The man had arms of steel, shoulders to die for, and being held against that ripped manly chest meant she could breathe in his incredible scent up close. And relive the kiss.

This all should have kept her in a state of agitation totally opposed to sleep. And yet...

Every time Dom had left her tucked in, her toes had curled with delight and she'd sighed happily off again into a deep restful sleep.

This morning she was embarrassed at just how much caring he'd had to do for her and how easy it was for her to let him. Totally not what she would have thought she'd feel.

Several hours later the phone call came that the newlyweds were almost home. Isabel had hoped her ankle would have improved enough so she could meet them when they arrived. To try out her weight-bearing, she swung her leg off the sofa and limped to the sink to fill her water glass. Not so successful. Once across the room, she dreaded the trip she would need to get back again.

Dom rose from his chair, where he'd been engrossed in his computer screen. 'I wish you would sit down. I could have filled that for you. You had only to ask.' He gestured to the child, who was peering out of the front window watching for the car. 'Or Chloe would have liked to help.'

He offered his arm and, wrapping her fingers around the steel of his muscled forearm, she was left with no doubt he'd manage most of her weight easily. Yet still she wobbled. Her breath sucked in as he picked her up so easily, becoming so fabulously familiar, and nestled her weight gently on the sofa with a 'tsk'.

When she had her breath back she chided, 'You'll hurt your back.'

His haughty brows rose. 'I am not so poor a specimen.'

No, he wasn't a poor specimen, she repeated to herself as she sank back into the cushions and hoped the pain would ease with the height of her limb. Her ankle throbbed now and he put the ice pack back into place.

'Please leave it there for an extra five minutes.' A command she had to agree with as the relief was almost instant as the cold penetrated.

And yep. She knew. Dumb idea to get up.

* * *

Dom frowned down at the stubborn woman. 'I will take Chloe outside to wait. Will you stay there until I return?' When she didn't answer, Dom nodded, cautiously satisfied. 'She is too excited to stand still in the house. I will hold her hand until the car is stopped.'

Isabel's mutinous mouth made him want to smile but he didn't. Watching carefully, he saw the moment she reached for her usual serenity. Drew it around her like a trusty cloak. Pretending that she wasn't affected by his touch. Or his orders. He wasn't fooled.

Such a mistaken trap one could fall into. The woman wasn't placid at all.

Outside, they could see the Lexus coming.

Chloe held Dom's hand as she jumped up and down on one spot until the car pulled up outside his brother's house. Dom looked down at her. The child's cheeks were flushed, green eyes shining with excitement, but obediently she waited until the car stopped and the road was safe. As soon as Dom let go of the child's hand she flew out of the gate and crossed to her mother, who had leapt from the car and wrapped her arms around her as if they had been away for a year, not two nights.

The way Teresa had wrapped her arms around

Tomas. The memory was bittersweet but precious. He was changing.

Chloe's sweet voice carried back to Dom. 'I missed you. We had an exciting time,' she added. 'Uncle Dom carried Aunty Izzy and put her in the police car.' Then, as if remembering her manners, 'Did you have a nice time?'

Rai met his gaze and his brows lifted, as did his mouth in a smile. It did sound quite spectacular put like that. Dom acknowledged the truth with a nod and thought wistfully that his brother had found a wonderful family.

Faith hugged her daughter. 'Yes, darling, but we're sorry to hear that Aunty Izzy was hurt.'

Dom walked across to Rai and they shook hands in greeting. 'She is much better this morning.'

Chloe prattled on. 'Uncle Dom has been looking after us. I've been showing him where everything is in the house.'

'What a clever girl.' Faith smiled and cuddled her daughter to her again. She looked up at him. 'How have you managed her, Dom? Has she been this excited the whole time?'

'Chloe is a credit to you, Faith. A lovely child and very helpful.'

Rai said, 'And Isabel?'

He looked at his brother. 'Isabel does not like being an invalid, but the ice and compression has repaired some of her ankle strain. If she would stay off it. This morning she said her headache has gone.'

Behind him he felt—hadn't heard, yet sensed—the approach of Isabel.

He turned and there she was, the crutches supporting her body weight off her injured ankle somewhat precariously. 'You could not wait until Faith came to you?'

She assumed her tranquil guise. 'I appreciate your suggestion, Dom, but I'm fine. Hello, dear Faith.' She leaned over and kissed her niece's cheek, offered that smile Dom looked for. 'You look happy.'

'As she should,' Rai said as he too leaned down to cheek Isabel's cheek. 'She has been cossetted and spoiled by her new husband.'

'Lucky woman,' Isabel teased but her face had pulled into the expression Dom had come to realise was Isabel masking pain. 'Chloe and I have also been well cared for.'

'Are you sure your ankle feels fine?' Dom couldn't help himself.

'I wanted to come out and join the welcoming party.' He noted she didn't answer the question.

'Then perhaps I should have brought out a chair,' he almost growled. Foolishness. Stubborn woman.

'What a lovely idea,' she agreed equably. 'But

not necessary. Now that I've seen the arrival, I'll leave you all. Faith can visit me when she's settled.'

She waved at Chloe's head, bent against her mother's middle. 'Chloe has packed her bag ready to come home. You can pick it up later. I'll go back and pop my leg up.'

Dom raised his hand at his brother. 'Welcome home.' But his eyes were for Isabel. 'I will help you up the steps.'

She took his arm and he felt the weight she tried to keep off her ankle. She limped badly. He huffed out his disgust, took the crutches from her and handed them to his brother, then picked her up.

Isabel hissed, 'Put me down.'

'No.'

Neither looked back as she was carried back inside. Dom could hear his brother laughing behind him and Faith admonishing him to silence. He was pleased they didn't bring the crutches in just then.

He thought when he had her resting on the sofa that she would berate him.

Instead, she turned to face away. 'You were right. Walking down the steps outside hurt too much to be worth it.'

And his ire fled. It appeared she was more

annoyed with herself than with him. He'd held back the frustration he wanted to direct at her for causing herself such pain but instead he blew the breath out. 'You know it will heal quickly if you let it. Would you like to lie on your bed for half an hour and I will put ice on your leg?'

'Thank you.'

He realised it must be extremely painful for her to agree so easily. 'Perhaps you require some medication for the discomfort?'

She turned towards him and smiled, though the smile was crooked and showed strain. 'I don't know that I deserve something after that foolishness.'

He bent, slid his arms around the now familiar curves of Isabel and lifted her from the sofa where he'd just placed her. She felt good in his arms. Wonderful. Not only because it needed to be done. He felt the tension inside his chest loosen. They had formed a rapport between them then.

'Perhaps if I was in your place I would do the same.'

She rolled her eyes. 'Right.'

Isabel lay on the bed where Dom had propped her, let the gentle relief of the mild analgesia he'd given her seep into her bloodstream and thought about the morning. She could hear him clattering around in the kitchen and she suspected he was making her a cup of ginger tea. Perhaps one for both of them, judging by the clunk of mugs on the bench top.

He really should go back to medicine because he was a caring person.

And a lovely man.

But not *her* far too young lovely man.

The sooner he was out of her house the sooner she could reinforce those thoughts. Wanting closeness with someone as damaged as Dom could be dangerous—though hopefully only for her and not for him. But it was hard to resist when he cossetted her so delightfully and in her miserable useless ankle state she could use some fun.

Though it had been embarrassing when he had picked her up in front of Faith and Rai. There would be some explaining to do and she doubted her niece would wait long to have a comfortable 'chat'. Probably less than an hour to wait. Isabel huffed a small laugh.

Living with Faith, and her single mother for Faith's teenage years as well, had given them a very close understanding of each other. Faith was the daughter she'd almost had. But now never would.

Dom reappeared with the tea and she turned her thoughts from that wistful subject. She inhaled the waft of aroma. Yep, refreshing ginger. 'Thank you. Just what I feel like.'

'I'm pleased. May I sit with you while we share tea?'

'Of course.' Didn't he always? He'd been in this room so many times tending to her she couldn't understand why he'd asked. But now? The idea made her smile. They didn't have Chloe chaperoning, perhaps?

Dom was such a delight to admire but she wasn't going to pounce on him. Or he on her. Sadly. No, *not* sadly. She was not in any way, even a little, disappointed with that.

He offered her favourite cup, the one sprinkled with tiny violets she'd bought in the Côte d'Azur, and sat on the chair under the window with his own. She tried to distract herself from studying Dom too much and noticed the one he'd chosen. The cup with the red fox, with a picture of the animal instead of the word. A gift from someone at work who'd been amused. She wondered if Dom understood the meaning. It was appropriate for her mixed and violent feelings about this man.

For fox sake.

Dom crinkled his brows at her unexpected smile. He was aware he'd missed something that amused her.

She didn't enlighten him so he added, 'Chloe will be happy to have her mother home.'

'Yes.' Isabel leaned back at the thought of Chloe across the road, chatting nineteen to the dozen to Faith. 'She's a charming child but she's a mummy's girl. Most definitely.'

'And yet her aunt is also charming.'

Was she? Instead of responding to this she corrected him gently. 'I'm her great-aunt, not her aunt.' Saying it out loud, often, reinforced their considerable age difference and made her feel more secure that she wouldn't be foolish over this man. 'You forget my relationship to Chloe and my age.'

His brows lifted. 'Age does not obsess me.' He paused. 'As it seems to obsess you.'

Dom continued, 'My brother tells me you have lived with Faith's mother, and then Faith since Chloe's birth?'

'True both times. They needed help to work and raise a child, although both would have managed if they'd had to. It seems the women in our family don't have much luck with relationships.'

He frowned, and maybe that had sounded too general so she continued, 'My sister's husband left when Faith was small. But I can see that Rai is going to change that luck now,' she hastened to add.

'Indeed. My brother is very happy.' He inclined his head. Looked at her with intent eyes. 'I wonder if you include yourself in that generalisation of ill-fated love?'

And she'd manoeuvred herself into this conversational minefield with her own stupidity. She sipped her tea to give herself time to think.

She supposed she could share a little of her background. In the broadest of brushstrokes.

'My one attempt at true love—more than fifteen years ago, mind you—left me abandoned by the man I thought would be there in my time of need. I'm not willing to feel like that again. My life has been happy as a single woman. I've travelled, loved it and made a living wage from writing and photography, and yet was able to be with my family when needed. I have friends. My family. Few regrets.'

She didn't mention the midwifery career that she'd dropped after the loss of her baby. She regretted that. She'd loved the wonder of being with a woman giving birth.

There was regret for the loss of faith in the man who had left her when they'd found out she was unlikely to ever be a mother. Perhaps even her loss of faith in all men was a regret.

Her inability to carry her own baby to term was too big a loss to call it a regret. That would take much finer brushwork than she was prepared for.

Time to change the subject. 'Faith tells me you and Rai were orphaned and lived with your grandfather as children.'

'*Sì.*' A sigh. 'That is correct.'

'Rai and Faith have that in common then. Being raised by another family member other than their parents.'

His face twitched. 'Not so similar. Faith had you.' He made an expansive gesture indicating all that she was. 'Our grandfather was a sadly bitter man.'

'Who took you in.'

'True. He ran a large pharmaceutical company in Firenze which I later took over. Raimondo was wise to stay in medicine.'

'Do you miss being a doctor?' she asked.

'If my grandfather had not needed me to join the firm I would not have chosen pharmacy.'

Which didn't really answer her question. He didn't say he would have returned to medicine, and she wondered why.

'From my perspective, you're a wonderful doctor. I feel very well cared for.'

He smiled at that. 'I am glad. But it has been too long to feel I could give all that is necessary to a wide range of patients. I would not be giving my best, as I would have if I'd continued in the profession.'

Ah. He'd decided he wouldn't be good enough. He'd lost trust in himself. Humility was fine but he was wasting his talents—especially now, when the number of doctors was falling. 'Don't you think a refresher and study would help? You have done some aid work fairly recently.'

'True. My brother seems to think so. But I have not been a doctor in Firenze since early in my marriage.'

Did she address the elephant in the room or back away? Backing away wasn't her style—unless it was from her own story. But neither was trampling on people's feelings. Very gently she asked, 'How long were you married before you lost your wife and son, Dom?'

He was silent and she thought he wasn't going to answer. She waited, not pushing him. He could answer or not, but her fingers tightened on the cup. She was hoping he would.

Finally he said, 'Eight years.'

Isabel tried some mental arithmetic. 'You must have married at a young age. Twenty or so? Childhood sweethearts?'

'Not at all. Ours was an arranged marriage… Teresa was the daughter of a business partner of my grandfather's, but we had known each other for several years before then. Early in our marriage I worked at the hospital in Firenze and the hours were long. When he first became ill, my grandfather suggested I take a sabbatical from medicine, doing only occasional shifts, and mostly I worked for him.

'Once Tomas came along Teresa was eager for me to do more normal hours and take more part in family life. Of course, after his death I took over the company fully.'

He rolled his neck as if to loosen the tension he'd gathered discussing his past. 'I'm glad I chose fewer hours when it turned out I had so little time to share with them.'

'Of course. Losing your family is something you'll never leave behind. It's not possible to forget but hopefully sharing the memories can bring you some solace.'

His anguish made her heart ache. And she had nothing to offer except stupid platitudes. She wanted to reach out and touch his hand. Offer comfort and support? Because she'd brought this on him, asking him to share his story, wanting to hear it for herself. Trying to understand why he had isolated himself from others for so long.

'I'm sorry to have asked. You don't have to talk about this…if it's too much.'

He shifted in his seat, looked away as if seeing another place and time. 'It has been almost six years. Then last month, after the fire…' He paused. 'It destroyed the factory.'

He had been through the mill. 'We heard that from Rai. I'm so sorry.'

'Don't be. That disaster did me a favour in a way, although it left me feeling…unbalanced. Perhaps I needed to lose my only purpose in life, even if it wasn't a purpose I enjoyed.' He looked at her. Hurt, pained and maybe a little embarrassed. 'Rai's wedding has been a very pleasant diversion from unpleasant circumstances.'

'I'm glad. You've added to the occasion by being here. We've enjoyed meeting you. When do you go back?'

'Christmas Eve.'

She'd been leaning forward, riveted by all he shared, wanting to be closer to him—not wanting to miss a word or a nuance of expression?

Isabel sat back, startled. Her hand lifted unconsciously to her chest as if to protect her heart. Protect herself from pain.

No.

Somehow she'd assumed he'd be here for another week. How had that happened? 'Why not wait till after Christmas? Chloe will be sad. You'll miss Rai's joy with his first Christmas as a dad. That's stupid.' She glared at him, suddenly angry with him. 'Crazy man.' Clapped a hand over her mouth. A step too far. 'I'm sorry.'

He looked a little stunned but strangely amused. 'I have commitments made.' He shrugged. 'It is a good time to travel. I would have left earlier, but Rai insisted I stay until he returned.'

He would do what his brother asked. But he was stubborn too, she realised.

Stubborn? Funny how that endeared him to her and not the opposite. But relief swept through her that he'd been brought out of his pain from the past and wasn't holding her lack of subtlety against her. Time to lighten the mood.

'Did he force you to stay, your brother? What a bully.' She tilted her head at him. 'Wait... I thought you were older than him.'

Dom blinked and then his shoulders eased as his mouth tilted crookedly, acknowledging her joke. '*Sì*. By ten minutes. He should show me respect.'

Discreetly she blew out a sigh of relief. It was good to leave heavy topics behind. Especially those she had instigated.

A knock sounded at the door. 'That will be Faith.' Isabel had no doubt. She'd be dying to find out how much Isabel liked Dom. How Isabel got along with Dom? How Isabel had managed with Dom's domineering presence in her home? She'd bet on all of those.

Dom stood. Took her empty cup. 'If so, I will go to Rai and leave you safely in Faith's hands.'

Isabel heard him place the cups in the kitchen before crossing to the front door. When he let Faith into the house she heard, sotto voce, 'Do try to keep her from walking about.'

Faith's amused reply was anything but soft. 'I'll try but I'm not carrying her anywhere.'

Dom laughed. 'My number is in Isabel's mobile, should my woman-carrying services be required. I will return for my computer before I leave.' She heard the door shut behind him.

Faith appeared at the door to the bedroom. 'He actually laughed.' She turned her head to the door he'd disappeared through. 'Who is that guy? Where's Domenico?'

Isabel snorted. 'He is less dark and gloomy. Chloe has really helped him, I think. She threw her arms around him the first night and he looked so taken aback and then gratified.'

'Chloe, huh?' Patent disbelief in her voice. 'What about you? Have you thrown your arms around him?' Faith pretended surprise. 'Hang on. You have. I saw. Your arms went around his neck when he carried you.'

And she'd known that was coming. 'Very funny,' Isabel said. 'Make yourself tea before you sit down. I've just had one, and I want to hear all about the honeymoon.' She considered that statement and shook her head. 'No. Not all of it.'

Faith blushed and ducked back into the open-plan area and the kitchen, which made Isabel smile. Ah… Young love.

When Faith returned two minutes later she sat where Dom had been sitting and leaned forward. 'So? Has he been carrying you around everywhere?'

'I have crutches, but the ankle still throbs when I hang it down. So yes, when necessary. My stupid ankle won't take any weight and yesterday I was still a little groggy and not so stable on the crutches.'

'You hit your head. Chloe told me it made you sleepy. I can see the bruise.'

Isabel sighed. 'I imagine it will get more colourful before it goes away. They X-rayed my ankle before I came home. It is only a sprain but it's driving me mad.'

'I can imagine.' She leaned even further forward and dropped her voice. 'How's Dom as a nurse?'

And there it was.

Amazing. Fabulous.

'Pretty wonderful.' Isabel kept her voice light, but the truth was there; he'd been brilliant. A hard act to follow. She tried a change of subject. 'At least this all happened after your beautiful wedding and not before.'

'Oh, wow, yes. And wasn't it just gorgeous?' Faith smiled dreamily as she thought back to her special day. She sank back into her chair and blew out a contented breath. 'I'm so happy.'

Isabel felt her chest warm with pleasure. Dearest Faith. 'I'm so glad. You deserve happiness. Both of you. The three of you.'

Faith sat straighter. 'And so.' She pointed one finger. 'Do you.'

And here we are again. Isabel managed to stop a sigh from escaping. Just.

'I *am* happy. Once my ankle is healed I'll go back to travelling. I cannot wait.'

Faith's face fell.

Oops. Not tactful or what she'd meant but it was too late.

'We have cramped your style, haven't we, Chloe and I? I don't know how I would have managed without you.'

No, that was exactly what she didn't mean. 'Good grief, Faith. You would have managed fine. Don't be silly. I wouldn't have missed the last five years for a million Qantas Frequent Flyer points. I've loved sharing Chloe's early years and will be rushing home to my own little house between jaunts.' She held her niece's gaze. 'No more of that nonsense. Please.'

'I'm sorry. Thank you.' Mollified, it seemed it was Faith's turn to change the subject. 'Do you think Dom will go back to Italy in a better frame of mind after being here?'

'I think that's possible. He still has two days with you all when he moves back tonight.'

Faith shook her head. 'But he's not. Moving back with us. Didn't you know? He refused to stay when we came back. Newly married couple he said. He's booked a room at Rose's B&B at the edge of town.'

Isabel grimaced. She could feel her own recoil from the idea of Dom staying away down the street when he needed to be with family. The man was determined to isolate himself.

'That's ridiculous. He only has two nights left and he needs to spend it with you guys.'

'Exactly what I said.' An amused glint in Faith's eye made Isabel lean back warily against the pillows. 'You could convince him to stay with you here, if you didn't mind. You've got Chloe's room free now if he could cope with sleeping in a single bed. Pretend you need him?'

Pretend she needed him? She'd do no such thing.

'I'm not telling fibs for you.' But the man was hopeless at caring for himself. He needed his family, especially now he was finally moving towards recovery from his grief. But it wasn't her place to put him up. Yet an inner voice suggested he was already here. She could ask him. No.

Faith pushed. 'That's if you wouldn't mind him sleeping in the cottage without supervision now Chloe's gone...?'

'Don't be silly.' A chaperone? As if she and Dom needed a watcher. Good grief. She was pretty sure a five-year-old wasn't observant either in that regard.

'Just a thought,' Faith said innocently and sipped her tea.

When Dom walked into his brother's house, Rai winked at him. Dom's brows lifted mockingly. 'A facial tic after only two days' marriage, brother?'

Rai's startled laugh turned into a big grin. '*Sì.* Excellent joke. My brother is back?'

'Accidenti!' The most polite swear-word he could think of. First Isabel and now his brother, shocked that he had made a joke.

Rai continued, 'So you carry the lovely Isabel everywhere now?'

'I carry Isabel when she is foolish. Which she does not choose to be too often.'

'Chloe tells us the motorbike whizzed past all of you very fast and smashed on the pole.'

Dom flinched. Felt his stomach clench at the remembered fear. '*Sì*. Too close.'

Rai stepped forward and he knew he had seen his distress. He touched his shoulder. 'It was meant for you to be here then, Dom. Thank you for keeping Chloe and Isabel safe.'

Dom itched to divert the attention from himself and to lose the thoughts of Isabel's near miss. That was too much. 'How was your honeymoon?'

A pause and then his brother allowed the change of topic. 'Short but no less perfect. My wife and I are very happy.' Rai clapped him on the shoulder meaningfully. 'It would be good to see you happy too.'

Dom shrugged. There was no answer to that. Yet. 'I must pack. Your house is an excellent dwelling, but I am still moving out for the next two nights.'

'Ridiculous. Stay here. We have many rooms. Or stay across the road and care for Isabel?'

'I will come often. But I will sleep at the small accommodation I spoke about last week. We have had this discussion.'

Rai tilted his head and a sorrowful expression crossed his face. 'What of Isabel? How will she manage?'

Dom narrowed his eyes at him. 'I'm here if Isabel needs me. I believe she is desirous of her independence.' He looked around as if something was missing. 'And Chloe?' Dom smiled. 'You have been home for an hour and have lost her already?'

'There are three ships close on the horizon and she is with her telescope.'

'Then I too will see the ships on my way to my packing.'

'Running away, brother?' Rai's voice followed him up the stairs.

'*Sì.*'

By the time Faith left for her own house, Isabel was sick of resting on her bed with her leg up. She needed to get to the bathroom after all the tea she'd consumed this morning.

The knock at the door, a firm Dom-sounding knock, signalled the return of her nemesis and she called out to him to enter as she slid her feet out of the bed.

'Are you going somewhere?' His question sounded slightly amused as he appeared at her door.

'To the bathroom. And no, I don't want help.'

His brows went up. 'I've come for my computer. Can I do anything else for you before I leave?'

'No. And I'm feeling cross so you'd best hurry away.'

He leant his big frame on the doorframe. 'Cross? Isabel? Is that possible?'

She huffed out a sigh and laughed unwillingly as she straightened and balanced. 'I've just realised I'm stuck here for days until the blasted ankle gets better. And I can't believe you're going across town to sleep and not across the road to your brother.'

'I have no wish to invade the privacy of newly-weds.'

He watched her, leaning on the door, all nonchalant gorgeous male whom she could ask to stay with her. Easily. As a favour to him. To Rai. It wasn't as if she was a young woman with a reputation to guard. But still, it was an awkward thing to say out loud.

He strode into the room and stood beside her, not touching. Just there if she needed him and, despite the frown she gave him, she was glad of his presence. She concentrated on her hands and feet, avoiding the other thoughts that were distracting her.

'I don't seem to have a walking-with-crutches synapse in my brain. It's still tricky to balance on the wooden pegs.' She shook her head at him as she manoeuvred herself towards the bathroom. 'I need to get used to these,' she said, pausing for a break. 'As for staying across the road. There's a five-year-old child living in the house. I doubt you're going to cramp their style.'

He didn't take his eyes off her and moved beside her to the bathroom. 'And yet I shall leave them.'

'You could stay here.' The words were out. She hadn't intended to say them but there they were, spread between them like unopened letter bombs, and she waited with bated breath for him to answer. Now she was terrified she'd encouraged him to think she was asking him to take their odd relationship to the next level. 'Chloe's bedroom is free.' A throwaway comment that almost sounded mocking, but she was mocking her own rollercoaster emotions not him.

'Such a gracious invitation.'

It hadn't been, as well he knew. That made her smile. He made her smile. 'Yes, well. It's only a single bed.'

'It's very kind of you to offer,' Dom said with a slight brow raise. 'Are you sure you wish for a guest?'

No. And not this one in her house for another two nights. Alone with her. Tempting her. Sharing space and feelings. Telling herself she was crazy, she turned her head to look at him but swayed with the loss of concentration and he put a hand out. 'Steady.'

The swaying stopped. 'I'm fine.' Now. 'Thank you.' Good that she had her balance back. Falling at his feet wasn't an option.

'I have made a booking for a room.'

She looked up. Met his gaze. Held it. 'You shouldn't go and stay with strangers.' This she meant. 'Stay as long as you like…' she forced a smile '…but don't bully me when you see me limping around.'

She closed the door in his face.

When she came out five minutes later her bed was pulled back to order neatly and her new boarder was standing at the door to Chloe's old room.

She felt calmer—which was strange, given the circumstances—but that state had been achieved by a severe yet silent talking-to in the bathroom mirror. 'Faith has made up Chloe's room with clean sheets. I think she was planning on you staying here.'

He didn't smile but she was pretty sure he had an amused glint in his eye. 'I can work for my board. Perhaps bring you tea when you need. Straighten your pillows.'

'There's no need, but I was thinking that was a given. Spend time with your brother and his family. That's what everyone needs, with you leaving so soon. You'll be having your meals with them and Faith has promised to send over dinner for me for a day or two. I'll sort myself for lunch.'

'And you will sit here in a lonely state?'

'I'm fine on my own and my house is handy for you.'

'Handy is not what I think of staying here, Isabel.'

Then what were you thinking about staying here? The thought made her skin tingle. She wasn't going to ask him. Her cheeks warmed but silently she swung her crutches past him and went into the lounge room to sit back on the sofa and lift her leg up to stop it swelling. In truth, it was becoming less painful to hang her foot down for a short time.

Soon she would be better. He would be gone. Life would go on.

He sat opposite her in the big white armchair he'd slept in the first night. Another piece of her furniture he seemed to have imprinted with his personality. 'I will be happy to know you would not be alone if you fell on your own in the night.'

Poor, lonely Isabel. Pity.

That was all. No, she wasn't disappointed. Not at all.

She'd jumped to conclusions, thinking he wanted to spend time with her.

Isabel let her head fall back and she looked at the tall, gorgeous man relaxing opposite. She was an idiot to invest so much angst into this. 'I'm surprised you'd want to stay here when I'm so crabby.'

He laughed. 'Crabby? Like a crab, walking sideways with your crutches?'

'No.' She had to grin at the thought. 'Crabby, cranky, cross is what I'm looking for. I think I'm going a little crazy, stuck between my bed and this sofa for more than a day. I hadn't realised how much I relied on my daily walks and getting about on my own two feet. It's not your fault and I may even be glad of your company.'

'Of course. Perhaps I can help with this.'

You could be more gentle next time when you fall on me. A wicked thought. She imagined his big body lowering over hers. The heat. The scent of him. And if that didn't make her blush, nothing would. She resisted the urge to fan her face.

He went on thoughtfully, 'If your ankle is better tomorrow, would you like to go out? I can borrow Rai's car. There is much to see that I have missed since I arrived. You could guide me and lose your "crabbiness" with a little freedom.' His brows lifted innocently. 'Is that a word?'

'Crabbiness?' She laughed. 'Yes, that is definitely a word.' As if he didn't know. She'd come to realise that these Salvanelli men could drop most of their accent or language idiosyncrasies at will. 'Sounds like something I would enjoy for tomorrow. Thank you.'

'Then I will cancel the accommodation and mention to Rai and Faith that I will stay here.' He inclined his head. 'Thank you, Isabel.'

And she needed to have her head read.

CHAPTER SEVEN

WITHOUT THE COMPANY of Chloe sharing their space, the evening with Dom felt more visceral. Everything thrummed. The air. The ocean outside. Her skin.

No amusing chatter from the child like last night, while normal chores and meals were managed. Now that her shock from the accident had receded and her ankle had finally begun to improve, instead of going to bed to rest, they sat in the lounge companionably, but both aware of the other. She could feel something but it wasn't uncomfortable.

He relaxed back in her new recliner while she rested comfortably, her leg propped along the sofa, and they both pretended they were only chance in-laws and housemates. His dark skin and strong features looked far too good there, framed by the white leather. She'd suggested a movie, one set in Florence during the Second World War, to share memories of familiar scenery, but they'd paused it while he made another pot of tea.

Words slid out unexpectedly. 'I'm surprised it's so easy with you here, Dom.'

He lifted his brows with that hint of quiet amusement in his eyes. 'I have some social skills and practise them on you.'

Yes, he did. 'Thank you.' She laughed. Like a schoolgirl. This was ridiculous. 'I haven't watched a movie for a long time. I thought this particular one might help us find topics of interest. But finding conversation with you is easy.'

She'd thought it would be awkward but any silence that fell between them felt right. Perfectly timed and not rushed.

Not just companionable. There was intimacy, their glances meeting when a scene from the film connected with them, or a place resonated.

Her cheeks had warmed and her body had thrummed. The last time she'd met his gaze he'd taken a long time to look away. Too much delicious connection and the first inkling of the loss she was afraid she would feel when he flew away. Hence the reason she'd suggested they press pause on the movie and have a cup of tea. Hopefully to calm the pulse of awareness that was steadily building between them like a distant jungle drum. Even her breath felt sensitive in her throat.

While he boiled the kettle and assembled mugs, she steered the conversation back to the reality of his leaving and needing to make a life for himself. To remind both of them. 'What are your plans when you return to Florence?'

'I must decide if I am a pharmacist or doctor.'

She hadn't thought there was much choice. 'Might be hard to be a pharmaceutical magnate without a factory?'

'There are concerns with that, of course. And issues that need resolving rapidly or we will all lose much of what we gained. But my priorities have changed.' He smiled. 'I am not the same man who left Florence, reluctantly, for my brother's wedding.'

Humour about his life in Florence. Excellent. 'Should you decide on medicine, will that be a hard decision?'

He looked at her, his scrutiny intense. 'No. Not now that I have discovered I wish to live and not just exist, which I fear I had fallen deeply into. I should follow a pursuit that draws me and not just diverts my mind.'

'So?' She cocked her head. 'Medicine?'

'Medicine.' He grimaced. 'But there is work to be done to be as useful as I should be.'

She didn't think it would be too hard for Dom to catch up. Fierce intelligence shone from his dark eyes and, except for the darkness he'd

dwelt in for so long, she doubted he'd ever had trouble remembering anything.

'Pharmacy would have kept you abreast of treatments, and you have had your field work to keep you credentialled. I think you're hard on yourself.'

'As my brother has mentioned to me.' His turn to incline his head and spread his hands. 'And what is your passion, Isabel? Raimondo says you work at the hospital.'

No. I was a midwife, but one day I ran from it because it hurt too much to watch others achieving what I could not. Women giving birth deserved better than I could give at that time.

Instead she said, 'I take photographs and write travel stories when I can. Meanwhile, office work has good hours, reasonable pay and I like the people I work with. I'll travel again soon.' It wasn't everything she wanted but it was enough. She was perilously close to lying by omission and she wanted out of that position. 'Lighthouse Bay must feel very different to Florence.'

'*Sì*. And beautiful in a different way.' He was watching her again and the heat under her skin was back. 'Your beaches are most amazing, with the white sand. I like the way the waves make everything fresh.'

'We have beaches with pebbles too. In other

places in Australia.' Her mood shifted again. Rollercoaster indeed. She turned to him and smiled. They both seemed to be doing a lot of that. Almost as if they'd had a glass of champagne. 'Though maybe not the same pebbles as you have in Italy.' No, now she was gabbling. 'But Australian culture must feel different.'

'*Sì*, but easy. I have been the one who is different.' He shook his head. 'Since coming here, it is as if I can see another life. One I thought I had lost. One I did not care to have lost.'

Yes. She'd heard that of him. And seen it in him during those first few days, and glimpses yesterday as he'd told her about his marriage. She liked this new man better.

'Why do you think that is so?'

'In Firenze, every time I was reminded of Teresa's death the guilt burned me.'

'Why guilt, Dom?' A big question to ask— maybe she shouldn't have. The last thing she wanted was to plunge him back into the darkness and pain, to see that other man he'd risen from. But she wanted to know, to hear the whole story, so she had to ask.

He looked at the silent television and she wondered if he would ask to begin the film again to avoid an answer. Instead, his gaze shifted to her. 'A small thing. But bitter. The morning of the accident, Teresa and I argued about my work. Teresa believed I was overworking, that I spent too little time with my family. It was a typical couple's row, nothing to threaten our relationship but a venting of feelings and opinions. I was to go with them. Instead, I stayed and worked.'

She said softly, 'I think you're being hard on yourself again.'

His eyes darkened with emotion and he ignored her comment. 'That was the last time we spoke. And I remember Tomas looking between us, a worried child with the quiet but hostile voices of his parents filling the room with emotion.' His mouth tightened. 'I struggled to come to terms with my wife and son's deaths, knowing that the last time I saw them alive they were upset…and I was the cause.' His hand gestured vaguely. 'I would have wished to make everything right.'

'That's understandable. And tragic. I'm sorry. So very sorry.' She reached out and touched his knee, gripping it briefly until their eyes met. Wishing she could take his pain and guilt away but knowing that it was his journey. That it was for him to work through them and forgive himself. 'Do you think Teresa would have expected you to hurt so badly for so long?' Her fingers loosened and she sat back.

'Something we will never know.'

'Of course. And you immersed yourself in the business?'

'My grandfather also suffered from the loss of Tomas, the loss of his dream of two generations of heirs. He died soon after and I became eager to fully lose myself in his world like he had always wished. I slept there most nights, but remember little of what I did.' He shrugged. 'The company thrived so I must have made the correct decisions.'

'No wonder your brother was worried about you.'

'Rai escaped to his aid work. I see now he had his own heartbreak. It's not surprising he didn't share his feelings about Faith with me. I was not interested in the love or heartbreak of others.'

The words hung in the air between them. Thought bubbles. Was that an intentional past tense? She hoped so. Quietly she asked, 'And now he has his family. A family you are part of.'

She thought of Chloe hugging him that first night after her mother and new father had left. Dom's look of stiffness fading to one of surprised pleasure and maybe, even then, cautious hope for the future. Yes, he needed children. Children she couldn't give him. 'I think Chloe had something to do with that.'

'Perhaps. She is a delightful child.' He raised

one brow. 'Or it could have been the aunt of Chloe.'

She wished. 'Great-aunt. Great-aunt,' she repeated as if it was a shield she could hold up. 'And that one's too old for you. You're a young man. I was just here when you woke up. When you go back to Florence, I hope you find happiness.'

'You are truly obsessed with our minor age difference. You are saying I could not find happiness here?'

'I'm saying you need a young wife, not someone over forty, to carry on your family name.' Oh, dear, had she just said that? Had she just presumed that this could be more than a passing fancy for him, a brief holiday fling as he started to find himself again?

He didn't rush into speech and her own words hung in the air, embarrassing her with a tinge of neediness she hoped he didn't hear.

'My brother has that,' he said finally. 'I would have a woman who made me want to wake each day to the promise of warmth.'

'Good plan.' She reached for the remote. 'No idea how we became so serious. Let's watch the end of the movie and then I'll call it a night.'

Oh, dear, oh, dear, oh, dear, she thought as the unseen movie flashed before her eyes. She could give him warmth but that was all. That woman he would wake to couldn't be her. But she knew inside she wanted it to be.

Such a virile man, with his future ahead of him. Though she had to wonder if her fear came from the scars caused by the last man who had left her because of her infertility, and not her own common sense.

But there were more reasons. It would be even worse if they tried to find happiness together and it didn't work; the ripples could affect Faith and Rai.

He watched her with a thoughtful expression. 'I will wake you with coffee and tomorrow we will drive in the sunshine.'

CHAPTER EIGHT

SUNSHINE ARRIVED AS PROMISED. Her family across the street had gone for last-minute Christmas supplies, heading south to Coffs Harbour. An added bonus was the annual family photo with Santa Claus. This year Rai would be included for the first time. It was a toss-up over who was more excited, Chloe or her papà.

After they left, Dom reminded Isabel about the outing he'd promised. As if she could have forgotten! There was no way that Rai would be driving away in Faith's all-wheel drive if he hadn't promised his car to Dom. Not a chance.

Isabel wasn't sure she needed to be in the confines of a car with Dom after last night's embarrassment, but she couldn't think of a good enough reason to excuse herself. After all, she had inspired the invitation by bemoaning her boredom with being housebound.

'Let us drive to the lighthouse to start,' he

suggested. 'I have not been even close to it and you can tell me the history if you know it.'

She knew the history. Backwards. Had been a guide there many times, preferring lighthouse tours to the local caving tours that Faith guided. 'You may regret asking me.'

Despite her misgivings, once she'd limped to the car at the gate, so pleased that she didn't need the crutches this morning, and was ensconced in the luxury that was Rai's new pride and joy, she felt fine. In fact, Isabel tried to calm the flutters that tickled with pleasure in her belly just from being with Dom.

His scent, his shoulder next to hers, his concern for her—all enclosed in the capsule of the car—were hard to regret. She reminded herself that soon he would be gone. Why not savour the moment?

'We can drive up to the car park,' Isabel suggested. 'From there, admire the external tower of the lighthouse.' Her ankle was better but not up to the hill climb just yet. 'Maybe tomorrow I can make the top, but it's still easy to enjoy the clean lines of the tower against the sky from the bottom of the hill.'

As they drove past the lower bends of the footpath and the row of bench seats that faced the sea, Isabel noticed a friend of Faith's perched awkwardly on a wooden seat beside the path. Something about her posture seemed odd.

Why was Trina out here alone?

'Can you pull over here for a moment? I want to speak to that woman—she's a friend of Faith's. You would've met her at your brother's wedding... Catrina, otherwise known as Trina.'

'Of course.'

The car pulled in smoothly to the side of the road and Isabel reached for her door as the car reached a stop.

Dom leaned towards her, concern on his face. 'Are you sure you are able to walk that far?'

'I'll limp and it feels secure with the bandage. I need to check on her. Her baby's due any day.' Isabel climbed out, careful to place her foot squarely so as to be stable. She could hear Dom opening his door so she guessed he'd be beside her if she stumbled.

'You okay, Trina?' But at the sight of the young woman's face she could see she wasn't. Catrina's face was pulled tight and tears ran in tiny rivulets. She put down the mobile phone in her hand. 'I just went for a walk... My waters broke. I've rung Finn. He's coming.' She turned horrified eyes to Isabel. 'Something else came with the flood. It feels like cord.'

Isabel's stomach sank. 'Catrina's a midwife,' she said over her shoulder to Dom. There'd be no waiting for Trina's husband. 'Dom's here. Let's get you to the hospital.'

Trina's wide eyes met Isabel's. 'I can't move, Izzy. Everything's happening.' Her face shone pale with shock. 'I need to push.'

'Can you wait a little?' Dom came closer, his voice quiet, the question hopeful.

'No.' There was a tinge of hysteria, so very unlike Trina, Isabel thought, and, oh, so very like the transition of labour.

Trina's hands flapped as if she didn't know what to do. 'It's coming. I'm trying not to push.'

'We'll move you. You don't have to do anything,' Isabel said calmly. 'You can't stay here. If baby comes at least we'll be ready to drive straight to the hospital immediately after. Finn will understand we put you in the car.'

Trina blew out a breath and, with several more panting breaths, she nodded.

Isabel turned to the man beside her and said decisively, 'Pick her up, Dom.' She had no doubt he was strong enough and wouldn't be squeamish at getting wet. The thought made her smile. Their gazes met, his startled but appreciative. 'I'll open the back door and put the picnic rug down on the seat.' She walked carefully back towards the car, glancing often over her shoulder as he gathered the pregnant woman in his capable arms.

The rug was more for Trina's comfort than her concern about Rai's car, she thought as she flipped the rug open and tossed it in. The soft cream leather would be cold. She turned to find Dom behind her with Trina in his arms and by the time he eased the trembling woman into the car Isabel knew they were going to have the baby.

'It's coming,' Trina whispered, and Isabel nodded, amazed the mum-to-be had found calm amidst the inevitable.

A baby born here would be better if the cord was first. Isabel wasn't going to give sympathy that might crack Trina's hold on composure.

'Clever baby. Let's get you out of your underwear.'

Isabel had her full weight on her good leg and leant against the side of the car. Between the two women they managed faster than she'd expected, and Trina rolled to her knees on the wide seat with her bottom in the air, her long skirt pushed half up her back, but she panted with effort.

'My word, it's happening,' Isabel said quietly. 'You are amazing, Trina.' Because, below the crease of Trina's buttocks, a glistening coil of thick cord was hanging down and the descending crescent of the baby's head with a stripe of damp hair was behind it.

'Head on view, keep going.' Isabel's words came from her past life. A life she'd tried to forget and now realised she missed with aching loss.

'I can feel it,' gritted out Trina.

Isabel glanced at Dom's face; he was watching them both with a furrowed brow. Then he said softly, 'So, were you a midwife or a doctor?'

'Midwife.'

He inclined his head as if something had been confirmed. 'Do you wish me to assist?' he asked quietly.

'We've got this. You may need to take the baby after, if it needs help…' The words *if the baby doesn't breathe* were unspoken but they were there all the same.

She, like Catrina, felt calm. Being with a woman at a rapid birth was something you never forgot, despite the passing of years. She knew this. Knew what to do. Believed all would progress because there was no other choice. Every second counted with the cord occluded and both of them now wanted the baby born here. 'Push, Catrina. Let's not wait for contractions. Baby is almost here.'

Isabel knew the mother was in a perfect position for rapid delivery. She and Trina both knew, with the cord jammed between the pelvis and the hard head of the baby, foetal blood supply and any oxygen it carried to the baby would be dangerously reduced.

The window of time for a good outcome was too, too horribly short, with baby's reserves falling dangerously low. A fast vaginal birth was the best option and even faster than an emergency caesarean if the mother was ready to push. That wasn't in doubt.

Leaning over the front seat, Dom slid one of Chloe's beach towels towards Isabel—he must have searched for practical supplies in the boot—and she took it gratefully as she leaned in through the back door. Wet babies were slippery, and the towel would be better than Trina's clothes to dry a damp newborn.

With a huge breath and a long drawn-out groan Trina pushed hard.

And pushed again.

The scalp grew larger as baby edged closer to birth.

Trina groaned low and deep as the baby's head finally eased completely into the world and then she gasped and panted.

Isabel soothed, her voice reflecting nothing of the fear for Trina and Finn's baby that curled in her stomach. 'You're doing so well.'

Trina puffed and then slowed her breathing

to gather herself. 'Not the birth I planned,' she gasped.

'But still amazing. You're fabulous.' Thank goodness her voice remained calm and steady. 'Keep going, Trina.' Isabel's gaze met Dom's and she nodded to agree it was good. Yet, deep in her mind, Isabel's brain screamed *hurry, hurry, hurry*.

Catrina pushed again. The end started with torturous slowness until, with a flood of fluid and limbs and coils of thick cord, came the baby in a rush—neck, shoulders, arms and body and limbs slid into the world and into Isabel's steady hands.

The roar of a car could be heard coming up the hill but there was no time to look.

'A boy. He's stunned but has tone.' A thick umbilical cord was good, Isabel thought in fragments of thoughts and exultation—the fragile umbilical vein and arteries would be well protected by the protective jelly inside a thick cord—but her gaze anxiously scanned the baby for movement as she began to rub his body all over with the towel. Not flaccid, some tone in his limbs was a good sign, but not breathing.

Catrina craned her neck but she couldn't see where he lay on the seat as Isabel rubbed. The new mum tried to shift sideways but there wasn't enough room. 'Still stunned. Let's give him a few seconds to start breathing himself, and if he doesn't I'll hand him to Dom.'

For Isabel, staring into the baby's dark eyes, so wide and blank, it was a jolt back to the past and another baby, tinier, a pale and precious being, who never breathed. Something else she could one day have told Dom. *No. That would not happen.* She rubbed more firmly. 'Come on, baby.' This was not surprising with the speed of his expulsion into the world, and his body was purple and not the white that she feared.

Finally, the frozen eyes blinked slowly and the small chest fluttered. A tiny mewling gasp broke from blue lips and, beside Isabel, Catrina sucked her breath in once softly.

The baby coughed and gurgled in a gasp. Then another deeper gasp and then a breath. 'He's breathing.' Her eyes stung and she blinked. 'He'll be fine.' She needed to say it out loud, for Catrina's benefit as well as her own. To let the words sink in and the relief and the joy to seep into her skin and mind and heart. The baby was well. 'He's good.'

She looked up to see Dom looking between her and the baby. Back and forward, his eyes shiny with emotion.

Isabel nodded. Blew out a breath and met his gaze for a second, almost overcome by the relief from the horror. She looked to the baby and gently swiped the pinking skin. Trina's baby mewled louder as Isabel wrapped him to stop the sea breeze cooling him.

'We've nothing to cut or tie the cord, so he needs to stay close to Mum.' She pulled her thoughts back to the moment, closing the door on that heartbreaking time years ago. 'But there's plenty of cord, Catrina, to allow you to shift.' Seriously—Isabel jollied herself back into a normal frame of mind—that was the longest cord she'd ever seen. Thank goodness.

Dom handed Isabel another clean towel and she unwrapped the baby and rewrapped in the dry towel, wadding the other for Trina to sit on after they'd disentangled cord and legs and baby so the new mum could twist and ease herself back until she could sit on the seat next to her son. Trina winced as she settled but reached for her baby, which Isabel passed across still wrapped in the new towel. Her face shone, streaked with tears, but her eyes glowed with joy and enormous relief.

Isabel smiled at Dom as their eyes met. Suddenly she was glad she could share this miracle with him.

A car pulled up behind them and Catrina's husband Finn wrenched open the other passenger door.

'Trina!'

CHAPTER NINE

HALF AN HOUR LATER, watching Isabel limp into the house, Dom could still not believe they had experienced a birth together at the side of the road. That moment when she had remained so calm as they'd waited for the baby to breathe… Yet he had seen the emotion in her eyes. A reflection of the past perhaps. He wanted to know why and how and when.

Today he had seen a side to Isabel that he had never envisaged. A capable, professional midwife. Was this not spoken about? Something he would find out today, he hoped. They wouldn't drive anywhere else that day.

'Enough excitement for one morning,' Dom said with a smile. He'd given her two mild analgesic tablets for the discomfort. Of course she'd forgotten her ankle. They both had. But she'd barely seemed bothered by it and hopefully the anti-inflammatories would keep it from swelling again.

He left her at her cottage to shower and change her clothes. He had no doubt Isabel would be ready with a strong cup of tea to share. Dom could do with one. They could sit and talk about their adventure when he returned, but first he needed to restore his brother's car to its former glory so he could concentrate on Isabel.

As he walked he muttered, 'My Isabel, you amaze me. And much needs discussing because there are emotions beneath all of this that I can almost grasp yet remain hidden. What are your secrets and your pain?' But he would be back soon to find out.

Finn had driven Rai's car with the precious cargo to the hospital, while Dom had followed in Finn's car to retrieve the other. But mother and babe were well. That was all that mattered.

It had been years since he'd witnessed a birth, yet during the drama he'd seen Isabel's direction of thought, the sequence of events and best probable outcome. Also there was the not-to-be-underestimated importance of the mother being attended by someone she trusted. Perhaps there was hope for his medical intuition and abilities after all, he thought ruefully, because though he'd been ready he hadn't felt the need to interfere. And his Isabel? She had managed as if this were an everyday occurrence for her. He knew it was not.

He stopped. Stared unseeingly as he wiped over the inside of the car, which had very little damage, and out to the ocean beyond. Struck by a memory.

Except Isabel had not been calm for that moment when the baby had been slow to breathe. He had seen an expression of horror. Remembered horror. And fear in Isabel's eyes. He mulled over that moment, thought back to the last time he had seen that expression, at one of their earliest exchanges of words, and he wondered now if there were big things she hadn't shared with him. Things he didn't know, that might explain much.

But again, that was something for a later time.

When Dom returned to Isabel's cottage he found her resting on the sofa, her beautiful face calm in repose and smiling. Relief flooded through him that she had gained comfort. He nodded approval. 'This is good. You and your foot have had a busy morning.'

Two steaming cups of tea sat beside the teapot on her side table. She must have heard him coming up the path and poured. The scene set for the two of them pleased his soul.

Her lack of disclosure about her past did not.

'You've been busy too.' She pushed his cup towards him as he sat down in his usual chair.

Dom considered the setting and the company. They were comfortable together, ready to share thoughts and opinions, except they were not in a relationship. The thought startled him and he veered rapidly away from that discomfort.

She said, 'Speaking of which, how is your brother's car?'

That made him smile. 'It appears to have suffered no lasting ill.' Rai would accept he had done the best he could. He gestured to her lower leg. 'And you?'

'Fine. But resting is nice too.'

She looked sad. Or pensive. And he considered the morning and the secrets that she hadn't shared. Her obvious expertise with attending a birth and the calmness and knowledge she'd displayed—of course these were not skills a photographer or a receptionist would have.

'So you were a midwife?' he asked.

The tea sloshed in her cup and he watched her frown at the small spill on the sofa cushion. Her hand steadied, she put the mug down, pulled out one of Chloe's handwipes and dabbed the spill and sat back. Lifted her chin at him with that composure he'd come to expect and admire from Isabel.

'The young Isabel was a midwife. Fifteen years ago. Her fiancé left when she lost her baby at twenty-four weeks. Stillbirth. She never went back to midwifery.'

It was disquieting that she had spoken as if it were all to do with some other person and not herself, but it explained much. But far too briefly.

'This is a sadness, Isabel. Yet you speak as if it wasn't you who suffered this pain.'

'That's not me anymore. I'm a different person. That was Isabel before. And, like you, she hung onto that grief too long. Until it changed all of her future plans.'

'Because your heart was broken? Or because the loss of the child could not be borne?'

Her mouth twisted into the sad semblance of a smile. 'Something like that.'

'You never went back to that man, I hope?'

At that she smiled, a smile that held a grim quality which made him frown. 'Any man, really. Short-term relationships don't require explanations.'

And yet she had given him an account, Dom thought with some hope that there could be more between them.

'What of me? I want you, Isabel. The passionate woman inside that I sense could be my soulmate. This obsession with your age and my need for a wife who will bear babies…does it come from this history? Your previous tragic birth?'

He leaned forward. Reached out and took her hand now it was free. Lifted it to his lips and said quietly, 'You are enough for any man.'

She stared, perhaps shocked, perhaps tempted. He hoped for the latter but then she pulled away and her face pinched. 'Apart from my age, which makes conception less likely and more risky, I have a bicornate uterus and it is unlikely I would ever carry a baby to full term. So if you ever changed your mind...' She let the sentence trail off.

The shock hit him.

Not for himself. No. But for this pain that he saw in Isabel. He ached with sorrow for her as her mouth turned down with unaccustomed bitterness. It was not an emotion he associated with his Isabel.

Her gaze slid away. 'Any man would later regret the limitations I bring.' She swung her foot down and stood. 'I'm going to lie down, Dom. You'll have to amuse yourself for the rest of the day.'

He couldn't remember the last time he had been dismissed. And this was not the time for her to leave.

'Isabel?' But she had turned away.

Finally he was seeing inside the real Isabel, not the woman who provided a calm haven for the rest of the world—he could see the pain she suffered, and yet she shut him out.

Dom watched her go. He wanted to call her back more forcefully but the pain on her face was pain he had worn himself, as he'd pushed people away. So instead he thought about her words and the emotions beneath them and her insistence that she did not hold false hope for a child of her own.

That, on top of the drama of the birth today and the fact that she had assumed responsibility for Catrina's baby's safe arrival, would have been draining after many years away from her profession.

He wanted to go to her. Hold her. Offer comfort. But he knew she would push him away.

He was leaving tomorrow. There was no time. It had been hard enough to be here for the wedding, with all that needed to be done in Florence. But a sense of urgency was building between him and Isabel and he couldn't help but think he'd missed the opportunity to break through her barriers if he'd just taken her in his arms.

Isabel closed the door to her room and sagged back against it. Today, like every day since Dom had arrived, felt like a wild rollercoaster that filled her with hope one minute and the next moment something would happen to sting with the pain of loss.

Even this morning, the initial anticipation of sitting in a car close to Dom for hours had swiftly changed to the fear and later exhilaration of Catrina's baby's safe arrival.

Then the closeness they'd found in simple things like drinking tea and debriefing together had suddenly broken her heart. All had been surrounded by the caring that Dom showed towards her in all of his actions. And now he'd said what she'd secretly hoped and absolutely feared.

I want you, Isabel. You would be enough for any man.

Well, she knew for a fact that wasn't true. Had found that before with another man, whom she'd not been enough for. As for Dom…

She'd seen forty-one summers. He only thirty-four. So young. So virile. She looked at the bed and waiting pillows.

She wanted to hide her head beneath the covers and cry.

But she didn't cry any more.

Had told herself to stop years ago.

When Isabel woke she found her common sense had reasserted itself. Dom would go home to Italy and her life would return to normal.

Of course it would.

Earlier she'd been overwrought after the danger of the prolapsed cord and then the excitement of Catrina's baby's healthy arrival. Only natural emotions after the first midwifery she'd practised in fifteen years, along with its unexpected drama.

She lay listening but the cottage felt empty. She didn't know how she knew, but the aura of Dom that she seemed to be able to sense in the air felt absent.

Empty.

No—this was good.

She would start being normal from this moment on. She would phone Faith and suggest they have Dom alone, without Isabel, for dinner tonight as he was leaving tomorrow and should spend time with his brother and family.

She would have a quiet evening on her own.

Yes.

She'd like that.

Ten minutes later Isabel put down her phone. Well, that hadn't gone well. Faith was making a family dinner, Isabel must be there, and wouldn't Isabel have months to have quiet evenings? Isabel could tell that Faith was disappointed Dom had been un-swayed about leaving for Italy on Christmas Eve. He'd reiterated that it proved the best time to fly without a family.

Isabel wondered just how many times Dom had scheduled flights or business to avoid Christmas in the years since his family had been killed.

He should be staying for Christmas. Someone should have convinced him to stay. She should have.

She shook her head. These were not sensible thoughts. And what about the one she was having now, of just having him hold her while she pressed her nose into his chest and breathed. To find the haven she needed and was beginning to think Dom could provide. Though she suspected that once he had his arms around her she wouldn't want to let him go. Would want to drag Dom into her bedroom and have her way with him. Like Mrs Robinson. Though he might be just as happy to have his way with her.

He had said she would be enough for any man.

Would she be enough for him?

Would her own dissatisfaction for what she could not give him ruin them both? And, by default, impact on her dear Faith and Rai.

Enough. Time to be sensible. To think of Dom's last night. Sensible thoughts would help her decide how to provide a side dish or a des-

sert for tonight, so she walked to the kitchen—
with barely a limp, thank goodness—and
opened the fridge to stare inside. The shelves
seemed crowded when she hadn't shopped for
days...

Then she understood. Dom. She'd asked him
to amuse himself. So he'd replenished her food
supply and then some, because he was leaving.

Typical, and kind of him. She wouldn't have
to carry grocery bags, something he would have
taken into account, she suspected. She studied
the shelves. Milk, bread, meat, vegetables, three
types of wine, soft and hard cheese. Fruit of all
colours. A balanced diet for the supposed invalid. Though she doubted she'd eat the olives,
anchovies and artichoke, peperoni and cheeses
in oil—unless she held an Italian night with antipasto for Myra and Reg.

No, she'd make that plate for tonight and at
least half of those ingredients would be used...
and wouldn't be left to remind her of the man
who'd supplied them.

She texted Faith, telling her what she would
bring, and set about preparing.

When Dom arrived an hour later she had the
splendid plate finished but her dilemma had
been it wouldn't fit back in the cold storage.

'Perfect timing, Mr Salvanelli.' Said breezily,

as if she hadn't noticed his gorgeously wind-
blown hair across his forehead, the curved steel
ridges of his abdominal muscles through his
damp shirt and his scent of the sea. Obviously,
he'd come straight from the beach, like a mer-
man out of her dreams.

No. She hadn't noticed any of that. Much.

'You look rested.' His eyes said she looked
good and she felt her cheeks warm.

'Thank you for the shopping.' Her stomach
tightened but she forced herself to say the words.
'I'm sorry for being a drama queen, Dom.'

'You are a queen.' His eyes were kind. 'As
for drama, I would talk of this more.'

She shook her head decisively. 'And I would
like to have a light, fun conversation with my
house guest. Let's leave drama for another day.'
Except they didn't have another day after tomorrow. Which was a good thing.

He inclined his head. 'Fun it is, Isabel.' There
was a wicked glint in his eye and she might have
just got more than she bargained for with her
stated house guest.

She looked down at the platter in her hands,
fighting her blush. 'Would you take this across
to Faith to put in her larger refrigerator, please?'
She sealed the last of the plastic wrap over the
dish and handed it to him. 'Now I know why
your brother bought such a huge appliance.'

He inclined his head, put down his damp towel on a wooden chair and took it from her. Stepping close. The heat from his body warming her more. His mouth kinked up. 'You know, Isabel—' his eyes darkened, teased her, invited her '—I too have a large appliance. Rai and I are twins after all.'

She blinked. Her mouth kinked. He did not just say that. Well, she'd asked for fun. Who'd have thought he had that in him? She snorted. She couldn't help herself.

'Does Isabel snort?' His eyes twinkled and suddenly their camaraderie was back. Angst was stupid and he was leaving.

Oh, Dom. You are a gorgeous man and I will so badly miss you.

'It seems I do.' Her shoulders dropped with the tension she'd held for what seemed liked days and her mouth lifted. A real smile. Throwing caution out of her seaside window she added, 'As this is your last night, when you come back from your errand we should sit on my little veranda and toast our friendship.'

There. That sounded very sensible and grown-up and angst-free.

He gestured to the fridge with a free finger as his hands were taken up with the platter. 'And I have just the thing in there. A glorious Prosecco I discovered in your little shop.' He glanced down. 'I will take this across and return for a shower if you do not mind the delay. Your seawater is a joy, but your beach sand sticks in awkward places.' He raised his brows. 'Unlike our beach pebbles.'

Isabel tried not think where the beach sand had stuck but she was smiling at the door as she opened it for him. 'I can wait.'

Not long later Dom held the cold-beaded bottle of sparkling wine and filled Isabel's flute, the swirl of the liquid mimicking the swirl of emotions he held in check. Another memory to take home with him as her eyes sparkled as much as the wine.

He studied her as the salty breeze stirred her hair to float like a dark halo around her calm face and he wondered how much it would be possible to miss this woman when he was on the other side of the world.

'Come to Italy with me.' The words came from deep within, not for the first time in his thoughts, but still he was surprised he had allowed them voice.

She laughed quietly and raised her brows. 'Just like that? Follow you across the world?'

She thought it was a joke. Better than a rapid, *no thank you*, he supposed, just a little miffed. 'Why not?'

She waved an arm, still smiling at his jest. 'Oh, no good reason. Just my job, my family, my independence. My plans to return to travel journalism.'

'All cold bedfellows.'

Such an old-fashioned word. This time she really smiled. Sipped her wine, tasted it and took another sip. 'This is a very nice drop.' Then she looked at him again beneath raised brows. 'Were we talking bedfellows?'

'It has crossed my mind.' He paused. Nodded sagely. Playing light-hearted, if that was what she wanted. 'Often in the last two days. Hoping. Praying.'

'And I thought you were such a serious young man.'

'*Sì.* I said praying. I'm serious about this.'

Her smile disappeared. 'Then no. I won't follow you to Italy. We barely know each other.' She lifted her glass. Gestured to the view. 'I like you. Very much. But this is a definite no. Drink your wine, Dom, and we'll go across and see your brother and his family for your last night here.'

'All right,' Dom replied in the same even tone she had used. 'We shall do as you wish, Isabel.'

And then he would make it his business— later tonight, when they returned home—to make real memories.

CHAPTER TEN

'UNCLE DOM, UNCLE DOM, we missed you today.' Dom's slight awkwardness with the child was still there but improving every day, Isabel thought. He had no choice because every time she saw him Chloe made a fuss of her uncle.

Isabel stood at the door and watched Dom as a slow smile creased his face. He'd hung back but Chloe allowed none of that. She'd raced straight into his arms and hugged him. Again, his hands came down to cuddle her back like they had the first night, when they'd all shared pizza.

'We had Santa photos today. Mummy and I have them every year, but this year my papà was *in* them!' The importance of that statement was evidenced by Chloe's out-flicked hands. 'Do you want to see?'

'Of course.' Dom had no choice but he looked genuinely interested, which was a good sign for a man who—according to Rai—had avoided children and family occasions since his own loss.

Rai leaned against the wall, watching Chloe, flicking amused glances at his brother and Isabel.

Chloe brought the Santa portrait over to her uncle. Isabel watched Dom's face. From where she stood she could see it was a gorgeous photo, but she waited for Chloe to come around and show her so the little girl could drag out and enjoy every moment.

The picture caught tall, handsome Rai in full grin. Faith looked supremely happy with her red hair spilling free around her face. And Chloe looked like the cat that got the cream.

'Even Santa looks good,' Isabel said, teasing.

'What do you think, Dom?' Rai asked. 'Is that a good Christmas photo or not?'

'Excellent, my brother.'

Isabel decided he looked remarkably comfortable as he nodded at Chloe's explanations of where the photos had been taken in the shopping mall. It was wonderful to see Dom so at ease, compared to the broken, stilted man who had arrived from Italy. A return to the world of other families and, she thought with a spasm of loss, another brick in the wall of her certainty that Dom needed a family of his own. Something she couldn't give him.

Chloe spun to her. 'Look, Aunty Izzy. Don't we look happy? And that's Santa in the red suit. He has a white beard, see? And that's his sleigh behind his chair.'

Who knew you would need to explain every element of a family portrait, right down to Santa's attire? Isabel smiled. 'You all look very happy, darling.' She looked up and caught the laughter in Faith's eyes. Rai was watching Dom and he seemed satisfied that his brother was fine with this.

'And there is my papà next to Mummy.'

And Chloe wasn't the only one who was proud. Rai's face beamed from the photo. 'You look dashing,' Dom said with a note of teasing in his voice.

'Of course.' Rai met his brother's eye and laughed. 'I am the most handsome of the two of us.'

'Funny,' Isabel said. 'I heard another version of that recently.'

And that was the tone of the night.

She wasn't sure if it was the two glasses of Prosecco they'd had beforehand, but there was no tension or doldrums in the Captain's house tonight. Dom looked happy and she couldn't understand how his mental shift had occurred so fast. It was as if he'd made a decision and she had no idea what it was.

There were some lovely memories from the last week and when he was gone Chloe would certainly miss him. As would she, Isabel thought with a hollow feeling in her middle. But, apart from having to care for an invalid and then being ready to resuscitate a baby at the side of the road, nothing had changed. She hadn't changed.

Rai said, 'We have your beautiful antipasto to start, Isabel. Thank you.'

'Dom bought all the ingredients today and they were begging to be put together and shared at a big table.'

'Well chosen, Dom,' Rai said. 'I have selected several wines to complement.'

That would explain why there were so many glasses on the table, Isabel thought. She'd be tipsy by the time they finished.

Isabel asked, 'Are we having a degustation?'

'I have a plan,' Rai said. 'With Caprese we will have Lambrusco to complement the tomatoes and basil. Chardonnay with the peppers and Pinot Grigio with the artichoke. Chianti with the cheese.'

'Stop, no more.' Isabel laughed. 'I'll be as silly as a hen.'

Rai said, 'You Australians. Cannot hold your wine.'

'You Italians make it a part of every meal. I have to walk ten kilometres a day to stay trim.'

Dom looked up at that and his dark eyes glinted with promise. Very softly so nobody but Isabel and Chloe heard, he said, 'I like silly.'

He was smiling, Chloe had climbed on his lap, yet he still looked relaxed and happy. Like a dad. Or a doting uncle.

The hollowness inside Isabel warmed and receded when he looked at her like that.

'Can you help me in the kitchen, Izzy?' Faith said and she nodded. A little time away from her handsome lodger would be good for her equilibrium.

Rai went to the table. 'Perhaps some Sangiovese rosé with the prosciutto, do you think?'

Dom took the small glass his brother offered and a tiny plate of the meat.

Rai went on, 'You look good. Happier. In so short a time. This place is crazy and has magic, eh?'

Dom nodded, not sure where his brother was going with this. 'I feel some of that magic. Yes.'

'And how are you after the excitement of the birth today? Did it make you wish to run from medicine or run back to it?'

Dom smiled. 'You are quick to see things. As always. I had forgotten the impact of participating in a birth. The drama. The exultation. And yes, it has directed my thoughts to the possibilities you mentioned before. A small medical practice between us in Lighthouse Bay is perhaps not so far-fetched.'

'It must be what you want. Not what I want, though, if that is the case,' Rai said quietly.

Dom lifted his chin. 'The baby could have died today, but didn't. Isabel was amazing, but I was there if needed, she knew that and it worked. The occasion drew me to think of things I had forgotten. Opened my eyes and my heart to my love of medicine. To the power of life and death with knowledge.'

'This is good.' Rai sipped his wine appreciatively. Took another sliver of ham. 'And Isabel?'

'She fights what could be between us.'

Rai nodded. 'They are independent women, these Fetherstones. Strong but steady. Worth fighting for. But if I can offer some advice in this matter... Do not rush her.'

Dom didn't say he was finding that hard. That this feeling of urgency warned him she might run from him with her absurd feelings of inadequacy. Which was ridiculous. Isabel was lacking in no way. But if he said so his brother would give further advice that Dom didn't want. So he said nothing.

Rai went on, 'Then you go back tomorrow. Sell what is left of the company and arrange care for the family homes in Florence. When all is arranged satisfactorily, you can return?'

'That is the plan.' Except now he wanted Isabel with him. The idea had flown into his mind and he couldn't get rid of it. 'I feel a healing. A great change in my life.'

'I am very glad.' Rai clasped his shoulder strongly. 'You worried me. All of us. It will be good to see you in the New Year, perhaps as early as February?'

'That is my wish.'

Isabel carried in the huge dish of lasagne with a rich aroma trailing behind her like a cloud. She heard the words and let them sink in. February. Dom was coming back in February. The idea excited her and made her want to sing. But that was probably the wine.

Her mood flattened a little. This changed nothing. The man needed a family that she couldn't provide.

To protect her heart, she might need to plan a trip away for February. But tonight wasn't for future planning; it was for celebrating the present. To celebrate and toast the newlyweds, Dom's obvious lift in spirits and Chloe's delight with the approach of her family Christmas.

* * *

The lasagne Faith and Rai had prepared together was a recipe that had been passed down through the Salvanelli family kitchens. Isabel, full with antipasto even before she started on the newly-weds' lasagne, felt the need to walk off her dinner. Plus, thanks to the excellent wines that had accompanied the meal, maybe dance a little if she wanted to really test her ankle.

But she'd been outvoted on that one.

After goodbyes, when Dom and Isabel crossed to her cottage under the streetlamps, the gentle susurration of waves from the bay filled the air. A warm breeze brushed her skin with a tinge of salty promise. With Dom beside her she felt more sensitive to everything around her, and because tonight was his last night the many sensations felt damnably bittersweet.

She glanced wistfully towards the sweeping light from the cliff across the bay and a longing to be a part of that ethereal landscape drifted into her mind. 'Let me show you the lights at night from the lighthouse. It's something you should see before you go home to Italy.'

Dom stopped and his gaze followed the moving beam of light that swept the bay from the tower. 'The path is steep. That is not a good idea for your ankle.'

She screwed up her face. 'I'm almost fully recovered. I'm sure I could climb up the last path to the lighthouse.' Suddenly she desperately wanted to go. 'Especially with the bandage on.'

His gaze rested on her, a little quizzical at her insistence, but he nodded. 'As you wish, but we will drive to the car park and walk from there. And I will steady you as we walk. I only sipped, while others indulged, tonight. Let me retrieve Rai's keys and a torch.'

While he went for the keys, Isabel slipped inside her cottage for a scarf in case the breeze turned cooler and a better pair of shoes for walking in the dark. But all the while, with an irrepressible smile perhaps fuelled by the dinner wines, she was wondering just how he would steady her. Hold her hand? Take her elbow like a recalcitrant child? She grinned at that. Perhaps rest his arm around her shoulders as he pulled her against him?

Enough. She saw the car lights through the windows and eased the door shut behind her with a click.

Dom pulled up near the gate and her heart skipped a beat. As if it was finally liberating to do something fun with Dom. Another dangerous suggestion, a moonlight walk under the lighthouse, and she couldn't wait.

Before she could reach the car, Dom appeared beside her and held the door open as he always did, protective of her. She slipped past his big body into the dim interior and of course the faint drift of his aftershave welcomed her.

She sighed as she slid back in the seat. She should enjoy it now because it would all be ending soon, this cosseting that had grown special in the last few days. It was not something she was used to, or had thought she'd enjoy, but Dom offering her old-world courtesy and care could never be unpleasant. *Unpleasant* was definitely not the word. She feared the word might be *unforgettable*.

In silence—an easy silence that she would also miss when he was gone—he drove sedately down their hill and up the lighthouse hill, past where they'd found Catrina earlier today. They shared a glance and a smile as Dom steered past. The conversation at dinner had been animated as the day's events had been discussed and exclaimed over.

Dom pulled into the deserted parking area of the lighthouse, dimly lit by one lamp at their level and one at the base of the path.

'Do many people come here at night?' Dom's assessment of the area was thorough. A man scanning for threats.

She thought it looked romantic. 'Not often. Though New Year's morning is popular to greet the first sunrise.'

He studied her in the darkness. 'I would like to do that one New Year's Day. Share that sunrise with you.'

As would she. Her cheeks warmed but the car was dimly lit. 'Hard, if you live in Italy.'

He didn't answer for a few seconds. 'Indeed.'

He opened his door and climbed out and she pushed her own. But of course he arrived to pull it wide and offer her a hand.

He took her fingers in his, looking down at her, not saying anything, and as she stood to balance herself he tucked her hand under the crook of his elbow, drawing her closer than strictly required so that their bodies touched.

His thigh was hard against her softer hip. She was well supported from any hint of a stumble, but strangely her knees felt weak. Silly woman.

His warmth seeped into her. As did the warmth flushing her chest.

His hand tightened and she lifted her chin to tilt her face up at him. For a moment she thought he was going to kiss her. The world stopped. And started again when he loosened his grip. 'Let us see this light.'

As they passed the cottages that lay below the lighthouse, once used for the keeper and the assistants, the steepest part of the climb had Isabel slowing.

Dom looked down at her. 'Should I carry you?'

'Up this steep hill? I'd have to resuscitate you at the top.'

'Perhaps. It is steep.' He laughed and she savoured the sound. He hadn't laughed when he'd first arrived, and now he didn't laugh often but his mood had indeed lifted.

He deserved to laugh, this beautiful man. A man who was leaving tomorrow. She couldn't deny that he had become more dear to her every day.

Ahead the lighthouse glinted and shone in reflected light from the massive beams that cut the night.

Surprisingly, with some of her weight on his strong forearm, her ankle was holding up well. She wanted to tell him about the history of the building but she didn't have the breath. She'd tell him later, she thought as she puffed up the final incline.

Instead, the light beams told any stories that needed sharing, the almost solid ray flirting out over the bay as it turned slowly in a wheel of light beams that warned ships of danger. And, fancifully, legend had it that the light also gave the town its hope.

Finally they reached the small courtyard in front of the tower and she leaned on the low white wall to the left of the path, ostensibly to look out over the dark bay and moon-tipped waves below, but really to catch her breath.

Silence stretched. Two people alone at the top of a jutting cliff. A thrum of awareness beat between them, drumming like the waves below on the rocks.

She wanted him.

She knew she couldn't have him.

But oh, how she wanted him.

She licked her lips and opened her mouth. 'The lighthouse is an octagonal tower. Apparently, it was easier to work the concrete that way. Easier than in the round formwork, that is.' Her sentences were short, but it was the pounding of her heart, not shortness of breath now that made them so.

Stay on track, she warned herself. 'It was one of the last to be built like this in New South Wales.'

His gaze travelled up the soaring height above them and he ran one strong hand caressingly over the still-warm white stone of the tower wall. She wanted to be that wall. To feel that smoothing touch against her bare skin.

He said, 'It gives pleasure to the eye.'

Yes, he does. 'I love it.' Not him. No, not him. But she wondered if she was lying to herself. 'And inside,' she said, forcing herself to focus, 'there's a beautiful steel spiral staircase.

Outside, at the top, the small grate veranda is black wrought iron lace, both floor and rails. The view's spectacular up there.'

'The view is spectacular already.'

They were in an alcove of the path, not much to be seen at all, except each other in the reflected light.

Not her. He wasn't talking about her. Her heart pounded again.

She moved forward, almost dislodging his hold, and he tightened his hand. Though now she wondered if for her safety, when they'd reached the summit and walked on smooth path, or his own desire to stay connected.

Either way, she was grateful for the darkness hiding her hot, hot cheeks. 'Come and sit beneath the light. There's a bench that leans against the white wall and you can tilt your head back and watch the light turn.'

They followed the curve of the white tower until she took one step down to the viewing platform and there, against the wall, stood the bench. She eased down onto the seat and he sat close to her and released her so that her hand slid away. Before she could miss his touch he promptly captured her fingers in his and held them again. He squeezed gently. 'This is nice.'

Very nice. Too nice.

But she spoke about the view. 'It's the surreal impact of watching the light beam shooting out over the sea. Each lighthouse has a different sequence of light timed in seconds.' *Be quiet, Isabel*, she thought. 'It's a simple but powerful pleasure to watch the beams.'

'Ah, and let's not forget the simple pleasure of holding hands.' She could hear the amusement in his voice.

'You can let go now.' Isabel raised their linked hands and when he didn't release her she lowered them. 'I can't fall here.'

'This is a concern.' Said slowly.

Cryptic man. She frowned and he must have seen it despite the dark.

She felt his shrug, a brush of cloth against cloth. That was how close they sat. 'I had hoped you would fall for me, Isabel.'

'I could fall.' She lifted her chin. 'But I'm too old for you, Dom. You need a young woman.'

He shook his head. 'It is your excuse that is too old.'

She tugged at the hand he held. He held on. Not tightly but implacably. 'Do you see me as a callow youth, unable to know my own mind? One who does not know my own wants and needs?'

'No. Of course not.' She'd insulted him. She was so confused. 'I'm sorry.' So she prattled on about the lighthouse. 'I love the blocks of white paint and the blue trim in the day, but I think the night, with the light beams, is my favourite.'

'Hmm,' he said. 'I admire the tilt of your mouth and the directness of your eyes. And your hair.' His other hand lifted and stroked the back of her hair in a slow caress that spread goose-flesh along her arms. 'But not your excuses.'

She couldn't do this. 'Stop talking.'

'I think that is a splendid idea,' he said, and his hand cupped her chin and tilted it towards him. His mouth came down and gently brushed her lips. She opened her mouth to protest and he kissed her.

The taste, the feel, the pressure of him was too beguiling, too fascinating, too mesmerising to deny.

Please. And she gave in. Isabel leaned in and pressed her mouth more firmly against his and his answer came, swift and sure. Gently, his tongue swept against her, his hands sliding up her arms until they drifted to her cheeks. Cupping her face, his eyes were on hers as he supped from her mouth. 'So beautiful,' he murmured. 'So stubborn. So desirable.' Her lids fell, and his kiss deepened. She was lost.

Later, sitting on his lap, when sense had returned and she had been thoroughly kissed, Dom said again, 'Come with me to Italy.'

Her heart cracked. 'No.'

He tightened his hold. 'I want you to come.'

She looked into his dark eyes in the dim light. They were like pools of potent need, pools of passion, pools of forbidden promise. 'People don't always get what they want.'

He tilted his strong chin. 'Before Teresa died, I had what I wanted.'

There was no answer to that. And she understood that would have been his biggest 'want'. He wanted his wife back. He wanted his son back. He wanted his family back. Family. She understood that. Grieved for him. 'I'm sorry for your loss.'

'No.' His voice was quiet but intense. 'You are wishing I still had a wife because you are tempted.' He sat back and he let her fingers slide from his. Bereft didn't begin to cover the loss she felt but she'd asked for this separation. She slid from his lap to sit beside him in the dim reflected light.

Dom turned his head towards the sea, away from her, and the distance grew between them when only moments ago there was no distance, just the melding of breath and two bodies, two mouths fused in mutual desire. 'Perhaps you are right. You think I am not a whole man. You deserve more.'

No. She wanted him. 'You're everything I could possibly want in a man, but I'm the one with issues I can't seem to get over. You have your life and the chance of a new family ahead of you, Dom. With me you wouldn't get that.' She absolutely believed that.

His head lifted and his voice held a sternness she hadn't heard before. 'Why do you get to decide who or what I want? Isn't that up to me? What if I prefer not to have more children— would that be an issue for you?'

Isabel blinked and opened her mouth. And closed it again.

That would change everything.

She stood. She needed to think. Re-examine her beliefs. But not with him, so big and hot and kissable, beside her. 'I'm glad we came. And glad you saw the lights up here. It is my favourite place in the world.'

He rose beside her and studied her face. 'Think on that, Isabel, when I am gone. I will remember your face, here in the glow from the beams, my Isabel of the light.'

Then he turned, gathered her hand and placed it back on his arm to keep her safe as they began the descent to the car below.

When he switched the torchlight on for the path she shook her head. 'Please. The moon is up. I prefer the dark.'

* * *

So did he. Dom knew he'd somehow ruined everything with Isabel. Had he pushed too soon? Kissed too thoroughly—or not enough? Been too harsh on her preconceived notions of what was good for him? But time was passing and tomorrow he would leave. He wanted more than her kisses before he left. Needed to leave his mark upon her so she would wait for his return.

Did she not share the feelings that burned in his belly? When he had kissed her, she had leaned into him and opened her mouth—it had been there, and that sweetness had swept them both from this place to somewhere more heated. The memory made his chest thrum and his hands ache to shape her beneath him again.

She stumbled once in the dark and his hold tightened, his other arm coming up to steady her. Her breath shuddered in and he did not think it was from pain but from his touch. He had to resist the urge to sweep her up and carry her against his chest, but he knew she would protest and pull against him.

Why did he carry such intense feelings for this woman after so short a time? Yet in those few days she had been with him for almost every hour of the day. He'd watched her sleeping. Been witness to her fearless protection of Chloe and the silent endurance of pain because of that. She hadn't been bitter about the accident, though he would ensure the motorcyclists would suffer the full consequence of their dangerous stupidity. Isabel would disagree, he knew, and her fierce independence made him smile.

He realised now that he'd fallen for her the moment he'd first seen her at his brother's house. That first day after the flight and a woman who had refused to allow him to be distant and morose.

An unassuming woman hiding the delight beneath demure clothing and an unshakable calm. She had woken him from a dark dream with her shining strength and kindness, like the heroine in a modern-day fairy tale, one his small niece would enjoy. If only he could find the happy ending.

He'd been the male version of Sleeping Beauty and Isabel the handsome princess who'd come to awaken him. But she had demons too, though she hadn't shared them all, demons like the ones he carried, and he would have to fight for her. Fight for both of them.

When they reached the light at the bottom of the path he said, 'If you won't come to Italy, come with me to the airport?'

He watched her face, saw the hope, saw the loss of it, watched her struggle to keep her face expressionless, but she had no idea how clearly he could read her now. His Isabel did not want a long goodbye because she cared too much?

Finally she said, 'Surely your brother will want to do that?'

'But having you there is what I want.' He cocked a brow at her. 'I did not think you were a coward, Isabel.'

He saw her spine stiffen. 'Nobody has called me one before.'

'Then, if to drive back from the airport will not be detrimental to your ankle, spend this last time with me.'

She looked away from him. 'If that's what you want, I can do that.'

Dom could not sleep. His body ached with longing to be with Isabel in the room so close to where he now lay. At least now she would drive him to the airport, though, to be accurate, he would drive there and she would bring herself home alone.

He wasn't sure if his insistence to have Isabel there for his departure was a last-minute attempt to convince her to come with him, or his pathetic need to see her face for as long as he could before he left.

Even his brother had advised him to give her time.

But things happened. Unexpected tragedies. What if something happened to Isabel while he was sixteen thousand kilometres away?

He did not remember this angst with Teresa. Everything had been immediate. He was there. Until he wasn't.

With Isabel, he felt like picking her up and running off with her, but she would just tell him to put her down. He had liked it when she had been an invalid and he could care for her. What did that say about him?

Isabel would have an opinion on that. The thought made him smile. Certainly she would tell him to stop being foolish.

He turned his pillow and stared out of the window at the night sky. A beam of light from across the bay travelled across his window as if warning him to chart a safe course. If that course led him safely back to Isabel he would be happy.

CHAPTER ELEVEN

ISABEL LAY STARING at the pink ceiling of her room as the first dusting of colour reached to paint the horizon. Before the sun broke through, rosy light dusted the clouds, turning them pink and purple, gradually turning to deeper and darker hues. Like a soft bruise on the horizon—like the bruise on her heart from falling for Dom.

She'd left the blinds open last night so she would see the sunrise this morning, but this empurpled beauty made her eyes sting.

Dom was leaving. And he'd called her out on her reasons for backing away. Turning it back on her, making her re-examine her beliefs.

In two hours they'd drive to the airport and she'd be going with him for an extended goodbye. She shuddered.

Why on earth had she agreed? Because he'd called her a coward? Or because she'd wanted to be there?

Last night in her bed she'd wondered what she'd been frightened of. If she would still be this careful when she was fifty…or sixty. How many young, virile Italian men would ask her to run away with them then?

Would she have been so foolish to take what he was offering, revel in the moment and risk the consequences of being with Dom in what she suspected would be an explosion of unforgettable folly? And what if she did discover a wonder she suspected might change her for ever? Was she supposed to then stay with a man she barely knew, in a strange city across the world?

By then she would know him well. Biblically, anyway.

What could she lose? What could others lose? She wasn't sure about herself. But others? What if, because of her, he never came back to Lighthouse Bay? Could she do that to Rai and his new family?

No. She wasn't unfeeling, but she wasn't a martyr. That would be Dom's decision and she could always absent herself when needed if her presence was a factor, arrange times he could visit. He could come then.

When the knock came on her door, like it had for the last three days, Isabel sat up and pulled the sheet to cover the rose-embroidered

bodice of her thin nightdress. She patted the
edges down beside her like a sealed wall of resistance. Even she could see the symbolism in
that. But, in fact, it was more for her than him.
She trusted him.

'Come in.'

Dom had brought her coffee every morning—
glorious coffee, hand-made by a gorgeous man
coffee—and placed it beside her bed. Then he
would sit with her as she drank it. The best way
to start her day, she'd come to realise.

Today was the last day that would happen.
Even when—*if*—he came back, he would stay
with Faith and Rai.

Unless she broke a leg.

She smiled a little mistily at the ridiculous-
ness of that thought. And touched the wood of
her bedhead superstitiously.

As he entered she allowed herself to savour
the sight of him. Tall and commanding, virile in
shorts and an open-necked shirt, ready for his
jog on the beach. His muscled thighs and powerful lower legs covered the ground between
them fast and she couldn't read his expression
as he carried the coffee across.

Ah, Domenico Salvanelli, her big, dark-haired
Italian man. Immense, harshly handsome, with
his sometimes grim and always sexy mouth.
Dark, dark eyes that searched her face with just

a hint of suggestion and all over her body her skin prickled.

He smiled at her, but that smile held a bitter-sweet tilt this morning. When the cup he carried lowered to the small bedside table where he always rested it, he paused and swung to her so their faces were level.

'Good morning, Isabel,' he said as his face drew closer. He leaned forward and kissed her cheek. Then he turned his face, his hand came up to still her and he kissed her mouth. Firmly. She was too startled to protest. He stood back. 'I needed that. I am sad this morning.'

Her thoughts scattered. She clutched at her shattered composure like she clutched at the sheet and huffed out a small gasp of surprise. Said the first thing that came into her head to relieve the hot wave of awareness between them. 'I'm sad too. No more coffee in bed.' As if to reinforce that innocuous topic, she reached for her mug and pretended to sip.

He raked his hair from his eyes and threw himself back in the chair beside the bed as if forcing himself to relax. Apparently, her calming technique wasn't working. The wood of the chair creaked in protest. The man looked sinfully sexy despite his obvious black mood.

Fierce black eyes locked on hers. 'Pah! This is our last morning together in our odd relationship and I should be in your bed—should have been there all night, doing all the things I dream of with you—not holding this mug with a handle in the morning.' He gestured to the cup in her hands and she felt the prickles of her skin instantly glow with heat and languor. Graphic imaginings were easily conjured. She was so there with him. *Good grief.*

She tore her eyes away before he recognised her response. 'Stop.' Said with a semblance of her usual calm. 'I'll spill the contents.' She put the cup back on the bedside table. She'd never look at morning coffee the same again.

Someone needed to be sensible. 'We don't have a relationship, Dom. Odd or otherwise. And we've done very well to avoid doing something irreversibly foolish.' She blew out a breath before she lifted her head. Then she raised her chin. 'You helped me in my time of need and I helped you. That's all there is.'

His eyes were fierce. 'You are mistaken. Which is strange and unusual for such an intelligent woman. Silent sparks fly between us. The air shimmers and my body tightens when I come within touching distance of you. From afar I can sense your mood and emotions. That is more than boring assistance; this is magic you deny. But you have had walls of resistance set up for a long time and I will give you some space to think. It has not been long and I have asked a lot of you. Perhaps it is unreasonable for me to expect you to follow.'

She shook her head at him. Oh, the gorgeous arrogance. 'Perhaps unreasonable?' she echoed, eyes widening in mock surprise.

He brushed that away with one of his oh-so-Italian sweeps of the hand. 'I only hope that by the time I come back to your Lighthouse Bay you will understand.'

Yes, he was coming back. Her heart thudded hard. 'Have you decided when you will return?'

'I have things to arrange if I am to learn to be a doctor in a distant land. And I will need a job if I am to woo a stubborn woman.'

Woo? Oh, my goodness. He was coming back here to work. And to woo her? He held her gaze then stood as if he didn't trust himself to sit by her bedside any longer.

'I go to the beach to run off the need to lift your bedcovers and show you how I feel. When I return we will prepare to leave.'

Her front door closed with a decided snap this morning and she raised her brows. So, Dom had a limit to his patience and she'd pushed it. Not surprising. Not as surprising as how much she wished he'd lifted the blankets. He certainly wasn't oblivious to her.

She sipped her coffee with a swirl of melancholy and frustration and a crazy delight. They had done well to not jump into bed together because the attraction between them was there. Dom was right. It did spark and sizzle. She finished her coffee and sighed, long and loudly. Lifted the cup. Examined it. Looked at her bed. She probably wouldn't look at her covers the same way either.

The good news was her ankle had healed, no doubt due to the fact her housemate had been so diligent with ice and care and protection. Her gorgeous nurse, doctor, housemate, friend and almost lover who was leaving today.

Enough. Today was a new day. A new start. She laid out the clothes for the day. Opened her drawer and saw the thick brown travel wallet caught in a dancing sunbeam from the window. Lit with light. Glowing with promise.

Isabel opened her handbag and slid the wallet inside. Zipped up the pocket. Unwise and disturbing. She should put it back. But she didn't.

She'd discovered things about herself. She wanted more from life. And she would search until she found what she was looking for.

If a small voice inside screamed in a frenzy that he was there in front of her she ignored it. Placed the first bricks level at the bottom of the wall and began to rebuild her barriers against foolishness again. Soon the shrewish voice would be blocked.

Dom would be back and he would be over his brief infatuation with an older woman. It wasn't as if she'd never see him again.

It would be good to drive home from the airport, to prove her independence had returned. Then she would get on with finding her new hope for life.

Dom glanced from the road to Isabel in the seat beside him. He'd suggested he drive on the way to the airport as it seemed sensible for her to rest her ankle until the journey home. Also, of course, he hated not being in control and she knew that.

She'd agreed calmly. As she did most things, but only because she chose to. Dear Isabel. He was not feeling calm. They had been driving almost an hour and every minute reminded him that soon they would part.

This was what he wanted. To have her by his side. Always. He couldn't like the fact that he was going back to Italy with nothing resolved between them, but he had to believe that time would come. It was unfortunate that he had to consider how long it would take him to sort and ensure everything went smoothly in Florence before he could return.

But he would win Isabel. Next time he wouldn't rush away with unfinished business he'd had to drop for his brother's wedding. He would take the time to woo her and then they would see if she still resisted his vision for their future. It was a vision he would not have believed possible a fortnight ago and now he wanted it with an immediacy that floored him.

CHAPTER TWELVE

DOM TURNED RIGHT at a roundabout Isabel said
was not far from the airport and had to stamp on
the brakes to avoid hitting the vehicle in front.

A barrier of disaster lay strewn before them.

Instinctively his left arm went out to protect
Isabel as their seat belts slammed them back and
the car skidded to a stop a few feet from the rear
bumper of the car in front. With urgent preci-
sion he reversed their vehicle onto the shoulder
of the road, well out of the way in case another
car came through at speed.

He turned to face her. 'Are you okay?'

'Of course. Thanks to your quick reaction.'
She touched his arm in a gesture of thanks as
her gaze scanned the damaged vehicles. Then
she scooped her phone from her bag. 'This looks
bad. And very recent. I'll phone to make sure
the emergency services know.'

Of course she was calm and moving forward.
'I'll see what I can do to assist until they arrive.'

Dom switched on the hazard lights of Isabel's car and slipped into the smoky daylight, jogging towards one of the vehicles, which was tipped precariously sideways.

A pall of smoke and dust still hung over the vehicles. It had only just happened. Dom felt a chill of fear run down his neck as he realised if they'd been a few minutes earlier he and Isabel could have been in the tangled mess of metal as well. There were at least four cars involved. 'Too close,' he muttered, unable to imagine anything like this happening to Isabel. He doubted he would stay sane.

He ducked back to Isabel with grim determination. Opening his door, he demanded, 'Stay in the car.' Then he ran back to the nearest vehicle.

Isabel looked after him with wide eyes. 'Right,' she said quietly, not planning to obey. What on earth made him think she would stay safely cocooned in her car and not offer help when it was obviously needed?

But first she needed to complete the job at hand. When the emergency calls had been made and she knew help was on the way, Isabel opened her door and slipped out, bringing her small first aid kit from the glove box and a scarf she kept for cooler weather in case someone urgently needed a makeshift bandage.

A low, wailing cry came from the direction

Dom had run towards, and in another direction someone swore, low and repetitively. Somewhere to the left a small voice whispered for help.

She headed for the whispers, stepping over broken glass and torn metal. Her breath hissed at the strewn wreckage and sounds of distress.

She thought briefly of the motorbike and pole, but that had been minor compared to this. The tang of spilt petrol added to the danger and she could imagine how those trapped would be terrified of fire. She was feeling skittish herself.

The first vehicle she reached was a small blue sedan, skewed all the way to the edge of the road with the passenger side crushed viciously by a wide-based gum tree it must have bounced off. The left side of the vehicle had climbed the tree a few feet leaving paint and had then fallen, but it was now jammed against the bark. Even from here Isabel could tell if there was someone in the front seat it wouldn't be good.

There was no entry to that side of the car at all.

She moved to the driver's door but, when she tried to open the mangled metal, not surprisingly, it was jammed tight from impact.

From the damage, it looked as though this car had been hit from several angles at once. The windows were tinted and the sunlight awkwardly shining, but she could just make out someone with their head on the steering wheel. The figure wasn't moving. She tried the front windshield, but it was cracked into tiny broken cubes and she couldn't see anything.

She heard a whisper and she tried the rear door, again jammed and skewed out of shape by a blow.

The rear window had smashed inwards as if a branch or projectile from outside the car had speared it. Shards of glass were scattered in a circle around the wreck, jagged edges around the hole where the window had been.

For the moment it was the only way to see in.

A young voice—a child, she thought, no older than seven or eight—whispered in a broken voice, 'Help me...please...'

Isabel sucked in a breath and moved closer to the rear window hole. 'I'm here,' she called, quietly reassuring. 'Help's on the way. Don't move until they say you can.'

'Help Mummy,' the voice whimpered. 'I'm scared, and Mummy and Daddy won't answer. Mummy's bleeding and there's a lot of blood.'

Isabel's heart contracted and she sucked in a breath. 'I'm here. Help's coming.'

But she couldn't get to the child. Isabel's chest ached with cold at the possible heartbreak to come and she looked around but there was so much damage and devastation she couldn't see Dom to ask for help. He would be busy else-where. So much for her own advice not to move anything until help arrived.

'Ten seconds and I'll be back.'

'Don't leave me.'

'I won't leave you. Just getting something until the ambulance arrives. They shouldn't be long.' Ten or fifteen minutes at the most, but in that time a body could bleed to death.

She hurried back to her car and pulled out the beach bag. Most locals kept one in their cars at Lighthouse Bay, always ready for a swim.

When she returned she called out, 'I'm back. I'm going to try to reach the rear window to see your face.'

Isabel used a towel from her bag to brush the shards of glass off the car boot before flicking open the clean side of the towel.

Looking down at her fine trousers and shirt, she was glad she'd worn something which would offer some protection from the glass, although she'd have been better in jeans. Nothing to what she might find inside the car. She tossed the cloth over the jagged window so she could push herself up and peer in the back window, plac-ing her first aid kit close to hand so she could grab it quickly.

Setting one foot on the bumper bar and her

knee on the boot, she used a piece of the towel to grab the edge of the window frame and shimmied herself up.

Inside, blood splattered the roof, the windows, the seats. Splashed and dripping, pooling into dark circles on the floor like a room in a slaughterhouse. One glance at the front of the car made her look away. She swallowed the instinctive gag in her throat.

To her right, in the back, still strapped in his booster seat and seat belt, a young dark-haired boy turned wide tear-stained eyes to her. For some crazy reason she thought of Dom. And Dom's lost son. And how tragedy seemed to come in circles.

Isabel breathed long and slow until her head cleared and her breathing settled. 'Hello, there,' she said softly. 'I'm Isabel. Are you hurt?'

He shook his head and he seemed to move freely when he twisted to see her.

Gently, she asked, 'What's your name?'

'Lucas.' The boy blinked as if he couldn't believe she was there. She'd bet it looked odd to see a strange woman peering in through a broken back window. 'Are you going to get me out?'

'I can't do that, Lucas. Not until the paramedics come. But I can stay with you until then.' Something sharp was pressing into her shoulder where she leaned on the sill. And her leg stung where a piece of glass had pierced both towel and trousers.

He thought about that. 'Can you help Mummy?' Then a frightened glance at the passenger side, crushed around the unmoving body of a man. 'Or Daddy?'

Isabel suspected his daddy was beyond help. 'I can't reach your mum.'

'You could if you came in,' the boy pleaded, and Isabel's heart squeezed.

God, he must be so frightened. Blood dripped from his mother's hair at the shoulder and dribbled down the back of her seat.

Isabel didn't know what to do. She needed help. She needed Dom. He was a doctor. She had distant medical training but she didn't have the equipment needed for a trauma like this. 'I'll go and get help,' she said.

'Don't leave me,' the boy whispered and even more softly, 'I'm scared.'

Her heart squeezed even tighter. 'Oh, Lucas. I know you are. You're such a good boy being patient.' Isabel peered to the left of the boy and the vacant rear seat that she could probably squeeze into if she tried.

Would it cause any problems for the emergency services if she did? She could climb out again when someone came. Would it make things worse for the boy? For anyone?

Well, it would for her if she tore something major herself on all the ragged metal, or the car exploded if a fuel leak ignited. She didn't want to think about that.

It would certainly cause problems with Dom. He'd blow a gasket and say he'd told her to stay. Perhaps someone should have stayed with his son. She wished she could have done something for Dom in the tragedy of his loss.

But that was the least of her worries now.

She needed to think about Lucas now.

It would mean a lot to the boy and from there she should be able to see where the mum was bleeding from. She might be able to stop the flow until help arrived. And check the boy. He said he was fine but, for all she knew, he was quietly exsanguinating as well. He certainly looked pale.

The fuel smell seemed stronger and she guessed it was spilling from a ruptured tank. She hoped no one was smoking. The thought made her shudder.

Isabel forced herself to look again at the front of the car. On the passenger side she could see the man would be extremely lucky to be alive and next to him a woman with long blood-soaked hair remained unmoving despite the conversation going on around her. Lucas's mother's face rested against the steering wheel. Though, watching carefully, Isabel thought she could see a slight rise and fall of the shoulders as the woman breathed.

'You have to help us.' The boy was crying now.

She couldn't not. She pushed the first aid kit into the back seat through the window. With a last assessment of how she would land and manage to right herself, Isabel wriggled her shoulders further through the window of the car and pulled her thighs and feet after her until she was squashed face first into the seat next to Lucas. As she wriggled to awkwardly turn to sit on the seat she heard Dom calling her name.

Methodically, Dom had done what he could for the occupants of each car. Applying pressure to wounds with whatever he could find. Ensuring airways were open and breathing not hampered. That people with injuries did not move until they could be assessed properly by the paramedics.

More bystanders had arrived and after he'd told them he was a doctor he'd stationed one sensible person with each car as he'd moved between them, triaging until the ambulances arrived. Only one car left to check.

He spotted the final car, pushed to the side against a tree, distorted and bent and smelling strongly of fuel. He'd missed it, tucked to the side as it was; this was where he should have first come. It looked by far the worst.

As he moved towards it a movement caught his eye and with incredulous horror he watched as Isabel awkwardly propelled herself through the rear window into the mangled car and disappeared.

Madre di Dio. For a moment he couldn't breathe, and then a red mist descended and he bellowed, 'Isabel! No!'

Adrenalin surged and he sprinted. As he did so the pungent stink of petrol rose strongly and he noted the reek seemed to flood from under the car. Worse and worse. He had to get her out.

What was the woman thinking? *Idiota.*

He pushed away the white-hot anger at Isabel's foolishness in risking everything they had, and might have. Pushed it away to worry about later. For the moment those who were trapped inside the car were more important.

Isabel was inside that car, his mind growled.

For a moment blind anger surged again and he shoved it down ruthlessly. She must have had a good reason. She'd better. He reminded himself she was a nurse and midwife. Even if it had been years ago, she had been trained to save lives.

By the time he reached the wreck he had himself under control. 'Isabel—' it came out remarkably mild in tone, so much so that he surprised himself '—what is happening? What have you got?' He saw the surprise on her face from his lack of stress, giving him a grim satisfaction.

Yes, he hadn't panicked that she was in danger, not that she could see now, anyway. But they would talk later about this putting herself in harm's way. He could exercise self-control in some instances. He shook his head. Mouthed, 'Later.' Then said out loud, 'What do you need?'

Acknowledgement of the 'later' flashed in her eyes as she replied. 'Something to stop the bleeding.' That so calm voice. 'Lucas's mother has a large puncture laceration on her neck and it's pumping blood. It soaked my small pad and bandages. There are tampons in my handbag. A small red zippered purse. Can you bring them?'

Good grief. Her favourite saying was appropriate in this moment. He nodded, slid back off the car and ran to Isabel's vehicle. Rummaged, found, retrieved and returned.

'Here.' He climbed up the car and held the small purse through the broken window. The sounds of approaching emergency vehicles were finally heard in the distance.

He watched her unwrap the tampon, lift the veil of the woman's hair aside and slide the wad into the deep cut, where it soaked up the flow. He'd seen them used before, but for gunshot wounds.

'When the paramedics get here, they need to come here first. She's critical.'

'Of course.'

'And who are you?' Dom asked the young boy in the back seat, barely visible beneath Isabel's leaning body. His breath caught and for a moment the child looked like his own Tomas. Same age. Same dark hair and eyes. He saw the child who needed help and knew why Isabel was here. For the boy.

'Lucas.'

'I am Dom, Lucas. A doctor. Can you hear the sirens?'

The boy nodded.

'Soon they will get you out.'

'And my mummy and daddy?'

'Yes. It is too hard for us to reach and help them now, so we will leave them for the experts. Isabel will need to climb out for the paramedic to enter. Perhaps they will try to cut open your door. If they cannot open it easily they may help you go out the same way. Okay?'

'Okay.'

The sirens were closer now and Dom said softly to Isabel, 'You have done what you could. It is best if you leave the way open so they can climb in as fast as possible.'

She studied his face and he tried to mask the sense of urgency that almost overwhelmed him. What he said was true. But he desperately wanted her out of there as well. 'Come, Isabel. Let me help you.'

Behind him, the sirens ceased and he heard the sound of many vehicles arriving. The shout of people.

Isabel turned to the boy. 'I have to climb out now, Lucas. The paramedics will climb in.'

The child nodded despite the tears that slid down his face. Isabel gently hugged him. 'We will wait for them to lift you out and stay with you until your mummy can be with you.'

'And Daddy?' Fear saturated the boy's whisper.

'Daddy will have to go to the hospital.' That wasn't a lie.

Dom's hand reached in and he watched, breath hitched in his chest, as she wriggled on the cramped seat until she was facing the back window awkwardly. Her cold hands touched his and he gripped one wrist and then the other. With a steady grasp and her own upward pressure he eased her out through the window until she was lying face down on the rear of the car. Once she was free he picked her up and pulled her to him.

'You are safe.' He squeezed her. '*Dio*, woman. Are you trying to kill me with worry?'

'I can't believe you told me to stay in the car,' she said shakily but with a determined tilt to her chin.

'What can I say? I am a fool,' he said, still reassuring himself she was safe. To his relief, she clung to him once convulsively and then kissed his cheek. 'Put me down, please, Dom.'

He didn't want to, but needs must. As he did so, men and women in paramedics' jumpsuits pushed past. 'Do you wish to give them a report or shall I?'

'You do it.' She gestured. 'I want to be back here when they get Lucas out.'

He nodded. 'I will tell them what you found.' He pointed at the car. 'Go. Wash your hands and drink the water after your hard work, and then come back for Lucas.'

It took an hour for the emergency workers to extricate Lucas's mother from the car. When she was removed, post replacement fluids for the blood loss, she was conscious and coherent.

Lucas's grandmother had arrived and had taken the boy home with her once his mother was free.

He'd been promised to see his parents at the hospital. Incredibly, his father was still alive, though his crush injuries had caused many conferences on the best way to extricate him. Dom and Isabel left as soon as Lucas did.

Time was running short for Dom's flight departure, but they could still make it. If they hurried.

CHAPTER THIRTEEN

By THE TIME they arrived at the airport they both wanted to think about something other than shattered families and accident victims. Or Dom's distress at Isabel's actions.

When he parked in Coffs Harbour Airport's car park, Dom shook his head that he'd found a spot so easily when his flight was almost due. He observed the scattered cars and the multiple choice of open spots and muttered, 'Australia seems so under-populated.'

'Looks busy to me,' she said with a smile. 'But parking is always easier here than what you're used to in the bustle of Italy.'

'Sixty million souls compared to your twenty-five.' And still he'd found Isabel among them.

'Not the only difference between us.'

Yes, they were dissimilar, but he realised that, instead of finding their disparities, difficult he gloried in that. 'Differences are to be celebrated.'

At that she laughed, a little shakily after their morning, and he savoured the sound. He wanted her less bowed down by other's distress before he left. He wanted his last view of her to be a joyful one. So he smiled at her, putting all of the pleasure he felt when he was with her, what she meant to him, in his expression.

Isabel tilted her head at him like a small bird. 'Who are you? Where is the man who arrived two weeks ago? I swear you are almost playful.'

He could be.

Wanted to be.

With her.

She opened her own door. Of course she would not wait for him to open it for her. He flew from his own and arrived to offer his hand, requiring fast movement from his own side, a game she didn't know she was a part of, but it had become a game he cherished.

Once he knew she was secure, he put his hand over his heart. 'That man has been healed by an angel.'

'Glad to hear it.' She eyed him quizzically and opened her handbag. 'Can I have the entry ticket you were issued with, please? I need to pay for the parking at a machine inside the terminal before I leave.'

'So businesslike. You are killing me. Does it

not mean anything to you that we will be parted
for possibly months?'

Even he was surprised by the honesty. As if
the immediacy of departure—and perhaps the
danger and anguish just past—had released a
freedom he hadn't felt for many, many years.
He wanted her to laugh again. To smile up into
his face, because he needed to take that with
him. A cure for his own melancholy. 'What if I
go into a decline from missing you?'

'Then I would think you stark raving sad.'

He frowned. That expression did not sound
right.

Isabel had no idea what Dom was playing at,
but her brain hadn't shifted yet. That accident
had been harrowing.

She'd thought their parting would be all doom
and gloom. This was much better, if a little dis-
concerting.

He opened the boot and removed his small
four-wheeled carry-on case, mostly filled with
his computer. She had no idea how he'd lived
out of that during his stay, though of course
Rai had taken care of the wedding suit for his
brother. And anything else she supposed, as
they were of a size.

They walked together through the automatic
doors into the departure terminal, though at re-

gional level the departures and arrivals were very close, under one roof and separated by a glass wall. This was only the first leg, his short flight to Sydney, where he would board a larger plane for the international travel.

There would be several hours' wait in Sydney between flights, as well as that bus transfer between terminals.

She stood back while he checked in, noting the admiring glances sent his way from other women in the terminal and the extremely attentive check-in agent at the desk. Their scrutiny made her frown at herself because there could be no doubt she felt a tad possessive over the annoying Italian.

Did she have any right to such a response?

It was done. Boarding pass in hand, he and his carry-on were closing the distance between them. It was time to say goodbye.

She would not cry...she would not cry...

Dom stopped directly in front of her. Gently, he placed his warm, large hands on her shoulders, pulling her closer into his chest until the button she stared at blurred in front of her eyes. She lifted her palm and laid it flat on his chest and pushed until she could feel his heartbeat beneath. His chest was so, so warm. So hard. So Dom.

His hand slid up and his finger lifted her chin

so he could see into her face and what he saw there made him chew those beautiful lips in concern. 'Come with me to Italy. The hostess tells me there is a seat that will keep you beside me all the way.'

If only she could. In a small voice she said, 'I don't have my passport.' But she blushed and turned her face away as she said it.

He laughed with delight. 'You lie.' He lifted her face. 'You cannot tell a lie; you are hopeless. You did consider the idea of flying with me, didn't you?'

She couldn't deny the truth. 'I just threw the wallet in, a silly idea. Briefly I considered, but I can't do it, Dom. I can't.'

Silently she added, *I can't risk you being disappointed in me*. Like the last man had been so disappointed in her that he'd left. She'd survived that but she doubted she would survive if she failed Dom's belief in her.

His brow creased, his smile fell, and she feared she'd given him false hope with her inability to hide an untruth.

His hands slid down to grasp her upper arms as if he wanted to shake her. But he held her gently. 'Why would you do that, Isabel? Why would you take the action of bringing your passport, making it possible, and not make it happen?'

Her throat closed on unshed tears. She didn't offer an explanation because she didn't have one. And for the moment she couldn't speak.

It had been a last-minute toss from the drawer to her bag. Almost as if she hadn't wanted to talk to herself about it, let alone Dom.

She looked away, ostensibly to see that no one was paying them any attention, but really to try and think of a way to get herself out of this situation. It was starting to slide out of her control.

His hand cupped her cheek, bringing her gaze back. Holding her with his intense scrutiny. 'Is it because you too can see that what time we have should not be squandered?'

She pulled back. 'You're so dramatic, Dom.'

'One of us has to be dramatic.' This was accompanied by a charmingly European male shrug. 'For you are too calm and composed and sensible, my love.'

Her head shook but her eyes were caught. Captured by his. 'There is nothing wrong with being sensible. And I'm not your love.'

'I fear you are. Have I not said you are enough for any man? I would have you, my love, if only you would have me. For you have slipped past my frozen heart to lodge at the core of me. Do you not care for me a small amount?'

'No.' But it was a useless denial that sounded slightly petulant to her own ears.

He laughed. 'And I know you lie again.'

Her eyes stung but she blinked away the welling tears. She would not cry. 'Stop it. Please. Goodbye, Dom.' She tore her gaze free. She waved her hand at the X-ray machine and uniformed officers. 'Go through Security or you'll miss your flight. I'm leaving.'

He reached out and pulled her closer. Cupped her cheeks with his big hands and claimed her mouth. His lips were soft at first, with a tenderness that created an ache deep inside her. Isabel breathed slowly, savouring the mingling of breath, her lids fluttering shut as she allowed him a brief glimpse of her loss, until that drew the stinging back to her eyes.

Dom pressed more firmly, demanding, a hint of the desperate need she felt herself and those two needs entwined and flared like a cordite fuse of pure heat.

His breath hissed in and hers was lodged somewhere in her chest. Big, warm hands dropped from her face and he stepped away, the loss of contact shattering them both.

'Goodbye, Isabel. God willing, we will meet again.' Without looking at her, he turned and headed towards the security point, his footsteps quiet on the polished floor, distance stretching between them, his body growing smaller as he moved away.

God willing. Her mouth pulled painfully as she tried to stop the trembling and her heart pounded. That man kissed like an angel. Angel? 'God willing', he'd said. She hadn't thought of that and should have after this morning's example of the fragility of life.

Cold doused her like ice from a bucket, flooding her skin, her throat, her chest until she couldn't breathe.

What if something happened to Dom and she'd thrown away the chance of finding even the briefest happiness? All because she'd been too cowardly to risk upsetting her comfortable life. Too scared to risk the pain of being discarded. Too afraid to trust.

There was nothing wrong with being sensible. It kept her safe from pain when she was cast aside.

But there was worse pain than being discarded. Unimaginable pain if she threw away the only chance she had to be with Dom. She'd thought it was always about their age difference and her infertility, but what if it was really more about her fear of taking that leap into the unknown, daring to trust? Was she a coward?

He'd said, *'I did not think you were a coward, Isabel.'*

Too frightened to trust him.

Too afraid to risk her heart.

Too complacent in her independence to do anything that threatened her peace of mind. Proving to everyone that she was happy and fulfilled in her guise as the calm and serene Aunty Izzy.

Isabel opened her mouth to say his name, the word aimed silently at his distant back like a sliver of incredulous fear. 'Oh, Dom. Be safe. Find happiness.' And finally, painfully, she whispered, 'I love you.'

She loved him.

Now she found this out?

Idiot. She knew he cared for the woman he thought he knew, but he didn't know the real Isabel. He knew the image she projected to the world. He called her calm and collected and sensible when so often, deep inside, she was none of these things.

Yet Isabel could remember a time when she had been more impulsive, but she'd learned to rein those feelings in, until now with Dom. Since she'd met him she seemed to spend half of her time simultaneously terrified and half tempted, wanting to revisit the old impetuous Isabel.

If she was with Dom she wouldn't recognise herself. Would lose herself. It had taken her a long time to find the Isabel she thought she was, but Domenico Salvanelli had turned it all upside down. Which made her feel anything but calm and comfortable. But alive.

What if? Fear scratched her throat with its talons.

He'd be fine. *God willing*. The phrase he'd chosen chilled her to the bone. Of course he would be fine and she forced herself to turn for the exit.

An aircraft roared overhead as it came in to land. Isabel made it to her car despite her tears-obscured vision and when she did open the car door she slumped into the driver's seat, shivering with a tearing sense of loss she hadn't expected.

In the distance the thundering aircraft touched down and applied its brakes. Soon it would take off again and carry Dom away.

Her hand reached out to start the car and she looked ahead to the exit. And slumped back. The old Isabel would never have forgotten that.

The boom gates out of the parking area needed a freaking ticket; she had to go back and do it all again. Despite her wish to drive as far and fast as she could, she wasn't going anywhere.

She had to go back. The damn ticket. The pay machine to the car park was in the arrivals hall and she had to stamp it with her proof of payment before she could exit the car park.

Maybe she wouldn't see him through the glass as he waited to board.

Back across the expanse outside, Isabel entered the other end of the building, a place of luggage carousels and waiting relatives, but instead of walking to the parking machine she searched through the window to Departures and the faces of those staring towards the tarmac where their plane had just landed. People were standing, massing around the checkpoint as if that would get them away more quickly.

She couldn't see him. Which was good. She just needed to stamp her ticket and leave.

But somehow she couldn't make herself move to the machine. Instead, she drifted through the crowd to the wall of floor-to-ceiling windows until she found the strong lines of his back, his broad shoulders and the ever so slightly arrogant tilt to his head. Yes, there he was, none of his handsome face visible, tension in his neck and shoulders she could see from here.

He wasn't looking to the tarmac; he was looking back towards Security and the check-in area. As if searching for something—or someone.

Waiting for her?

What if he did love her?

And the voice in her head. Accusing. What was she so afraid of that she wouldn't risk finding out?

And it came to her, crystal-clear. Like spring water. A dousing of life and purity. She really did love Dom. He deserved to be allowed to love her.

Finally, the only thing that terrified Isabel on the deepest primal level was the idea that she might not see Domenico Salvanelli ever again.

What if something did happen and she wasn't there?

What if she never knew what it was like to lie in his arms?

What if he never knew that she loved him?

The first passengers from the aircraft on the tarmac began to stream into the arrivals hall, greeting relatives, children running, the volume suddenly increased as if someone had turned a dial.

The carousel for luggage beeped and groaned and began to turn with grinding slowness.

All she needed was a little more time to decide.

She could fly to Sydney and talk to him. Heck, she could buy a set of clothes in the airport and even a carry-on bag if she decided to go all the way to Italy. But she couldn't think of that yet. The parking bill would grow until Faith or Rai could retrieve her car, but that was fine. Faith had spare keys, could eat the food in her fridge, lock her doors, hold the fort until her return.

There really was no reason for her not to go.

Isabel laughed, turned and prepared to do the craziest thing she'd ever done in her life. To follow a man seven years her junior and offer herself as a lover.

Isabel spun, walked briskly out of Arrivals, down the footpath to Departures and entered the now almost deserted building. The loud speaker announced that boarding had commenced for the flight to Sydney and through the windows the scrum of passengers shuffled forward to offer their boarding passes and Dom was lost in a sea of milling people.

The agent at the check-in counter shot Isabel a quizzical look that said, *You're very late...or very early for the next flight.*

'Can I buy a ticket on that flight to Sydney, please? Heck, give me one to Rome. Last-minute decision. I don't have any luggage.' She smiled and it felt as if her face might break open with the sudden excitement that glowed inside.

The glow must have shone externally too. 'It looks like a good choice.' The woman glanced at her watch and smiled. 'I think we can manage that, if we're super-fast.'

Isabel already had her driver's licence and credit card.

The agent's shoulders drooped. 'Oh, I'm sorry. I knew we were cutting it fine, but I'm afraid it was too fine. The flight has just closed.'

CHAPTER FOURTEEN

SHE WASN'T COMING. Dom accepted he'd been mistaken to nurture even the tiniest hope that Isabel would throw caution to the winds. Though she had once been so brave, and his body thrummed with the memory of her glorious body against his in that last kiss. But this insistent dream and craziness to want her to fly across the world with him had been too much to ask and he was a fool to think she would change her mind at the last minute.

He'd maintained hope until the last few passengers came through Security into the departure lounge. Now he called himself an idiot as he crossed the tarmac and ascended the steps into the front of the aircraft. He stowed his bag above his seat and settled beside his allocated window in the small plane.

The cabin was barely half full. Only fools and family flew at Christmas. His business class ticket to Rome and then Florence meant the seat next to him was empty and he had room to stretch his legs. He opened his phone and texted his brother that he was on board.

The text came back. 'What of Isabel?'

Had Raimondo known what he was thinking? Had she shared her indecision with Faith? His heart thundered with renewed hope as he stared at his phone. The announcement asked passengers to switch all electronic equipment to flight mode.

The hostess stood waiting at the cockpit, a cardboard instruction sheet in her hand. She smiled at him and said softly, 'One more passenger and then we'll close the door.'

Isabel's heart sank to the cold tiled floor under her feet. Too late. She'd blown it with her indecision. Her inability to see what was crystal-clear in front of her eyes. 'Isn't there anything you can do?'

The woman looked suitably apologetic. 'Not for this flight.' She tapped screens and stared at her computer. 'There's a flight departing Port Macquarie in two hours. It gets you to Sydney two hours before the Rome departure and it takes roughly an hour and a half to drive to Port. It'll be close. You still might not make it but at least you don't have luggage. I can check you in from here.'

'Do it. Book it. Check me in. Take my card. Sydney to Florence via Rome.' She was mad. Crazy. Crazy in love. And in no condition to drive fast so she'd have to drive carefully.

She didn't stay to see Dom's plane take off. She ran to Arrivals and paid the wonderful parking machine that had changed her mind. Thank goodness she'd filled her car up last week and wouldn't run out of petrol with an extra hundred and fifty kilometres to drive.

On the way back to the highway the link road was down to one lane and banked back more than she'd expected. She glanced at her watch. She had one hundred minutes.

Of course! The accident!

She put on her indicator and performed a quick U-turn and headed a different way to the highway. Longer distance but moving traffic. Her head began to throb with the strain of the morning and the fact she needed food.

She grabbed her water bottle and drained most of it. Probably dehydrated as well with adrenalin. She kept twenty mils in the bottom. She might have to run later and she'd need a sip.

Glancing at the car clock, she worked out how many minutes she had. Halfway there and seventy minutes until take-off. She shook her head. What was she doing?

Once on the M1, Isabel overtook another

slow car and kept her speed legal, something she didn't normally have trouble with but today she was on edge. Thankfully, the new highway was conducive to fast travel but still she watched the minutes tick by.

She had to make it. Such a crazy thing to attempt. She would not think of that; she would drive, drive, drive.

Exactly one hundred minutes after exiting the Coffs Harbour car park, she rolled into Port Macquarie airport with a grunt of relief. Took the ticket from the parking machine and bared her teeth at it in a grimace of a smile. She could leave that in the car for Faith.

Striding across the car park to the terminal, she saw her plane had already landed. Passengers were boarding. That was okay. She had her boarding pass. She'd done it.

With a jubilant fist pump, Isabel strode into the departure lounge and headed for the security check. Through the window she could see the line of passengers snaking towards the plane. Still time. She couldn't believe she'd made it.

She placed her handbag on the conveyer belt and it disappeared through as she imagined Dom's face when she arrived in Sydney. A smile spread across her face and her heart leapt in anticipation of that moment.

Bells rang. Lights flashed. And Isabel's heart stuttered. Now what? Her bag reversed out of the X-ray back into sight and her stomach sank.

The tall grey-haired man said in a bored tone, 'You have scissors, lady.'

Isabel blinked. Resisted the urge to grab her bag and upend it in the middle of the conveyor belt. Instead, she forced a smile and followed after the officer as he carried her bag to the side table, where he pulled on nitrile gloves. With torturous slowness. She glanced through the window at the last boarding passengers.

This had all been in vain. The universe was trying to tell her something—via a pair of darn nail scissors!—and she watched the last passenger for her flight step onto the plane.

'You'll have to leave them.'

Isabel blinked. 'What?' Her thoughts jerked back from the loss of a dream.

'The scissors,' the man said. 'If you want to catch that flight you'll have to leave the scissors.'

In Sydney Airport, Dom accepted he'd lost. She hadn't boarded in Coffs Harbour. He'd been so certain that one final passenger would be Isabel. He'd been convinced she would appear. Instead, it had been a young man with a backpack who'd scurried up the stairs and into the cabin, and they'd closed the doors.

He raked his hand through his hair and swore silently as he looked at his watch. He had two hours to decide if he would toss his business worries, and a small fortune, to the wind and go back to claim Isabel. Or catch the flight to Florence and return to Lighthouse Bay another day.

He rocked gently as he squeezed the bridge of his nose between his fingers. His phone rang. He almost dropped it in his haste to see if it was Isabel.

Not Isabel. 'Rai. Yes. In Sydney. Thank you. Is Isabel safely home?'

His brother's denial made his brows draw together. 'Faith hasn't heard from her?'

Rai suggested, 'Perhaps she has gone shopping. The shops are better in Coffs Harbour.'

Dom did not think his Isabel would be shopping today. Thoughts skittered and hope flared. 'I am considering my return. Not taking the flight to Rome.'

'What?' Rai's disbelief carried clearly down the line. 'Brother. Do not rue a decision made in haste.'

Dom didn't like that. 'I am still deciding.'

'You have to return to Florence at some point for the factory.' Rai's opinion was clear. 'I appreciate your attendance at my wedding but we both know it is you who will lose a large sum if you delay much longer.'

Dom's chin lifted and he narrowed his eyes at the phone. Glaring at his brother, who had found his happiness and seemed intent on denying him the same. 'And yet today I consider returning to Lighthouse Bay, rather than boarding my flight.'

Rai's dissenting mutter made Dom smile. His words did not. 'You will be coming back to Lighthouse Bay within months. If Isabel is the right woman for you, she will be waiting. Give her time and space; do not rush her. She is a cautious woman, and an independent one. She needs to make her own decisions.'

Except Dom knew his Isabel was many things, and that he'd encouraged her to be more impulsive. To grab the life she wanted and the happiness she deserved. Who knew what that quixotic woman would do while he was gone? She might head off on a round-the-world adventure without him and he would spend years waiting. Would he risk that?

Isabel arrived in Sydney, was one of the first to stand up when the seat belt sign went off, but she was well down the aircraft and had to wait for those in front to alight.

Finally, she stepped out…

And there was a bus. Not a walkway to the terminal that she could run through. *Saints preserve her.* She climbed on and stood in the bus, holding a hand strap from the roof with white knuckles and a twisting stomach. Turning her arm to stare at the moving numbers on her watch. Finally all the passengers from the aircraft transferred into the bus. With all the speed of the slowest tortoise.

Eventually the bus started, moving at a different tortoise's pace, and then stopped, waited for an aircraft to cross the runway, before it headed again through molasses towards the terminal.

Five minutes later it docked at the terminal. 'Excuse me,' she said. 'Sorry,' as she bumped a man who scowled at her. Desperately she slipped between disembarking passengers and took off briskly in front of the crowd. Terrified she'd be behind a long line of slow movers up the escalators to the departure hall floor.

She knew the way. Had travelled from Sydney often and headed for the inter-terminal bus that would take her to the international departure gates. Seventy minutes until Dom's aircraft departed.

Dom's and hers, she corrected herself.

The doors were open, a bus must be near to departing and she quickened her pace. The attendant looked up, took her boarding pass and glanced at it. 'You'll be pushing to make this flight.'

Isabel sucked in a breath and felt the rush of tears. Forced them back. Swallowed as she took back the boarding pass. 'I know.' Lifted her head and looked the woman in the eye. 'The man I love is on that flight and he doesn't know I'm here. I must make it.'

The woman nodded. Handed her an Express Lane Pass for immigration and picked up the phone. 'I'll let them know you're coming but I can't promise they'll hold it for you.'

'Thank you,' she called over her shoulder and took the descending escalators fast to the almost full bus below.

Again, she stood swaying, holding onto the hand strap in a bus she'd had no idea she'd be travelling on when she'd woken this morning.

This morning.

So long ago.

So much had happened.

There was still a chance she would make it. No chance for clothes or luggage or food. But food could happen on the plane. Dom would happen on the plane. She would not lose sight of that.

Jogging up the long stairs because she couldn't stand quietly in a line on the escalator, Isabel reached the international departure hall. She headed straight for the departing passengers gate and slipped into the immigration and customs hall. The queues were staggeringly long and she almost sobbed before she remembered her Express Pass in her shaking hand.

She held it up to the border control officer and he allowed her past his gate, but still there were a dozen ahead of her with waving passports and she had less than five minutes until her flight boarded.

At least she no longer had the scissors to hold her up when she made it to the X-ray machines.

Except they waved her across to the random explosives test. She almost laughed with hysteria. The officer studied her strange facial tic with suspicion, and she waved her hand at the flashing lights overhead. 'The departures board is flashing "Boarding" next to my flight number.'

Totally unmoved, the man offered his obviously standard answer. 'This won't take a moment.'

Isabel bit back the caustic reply that it didn't take long to shut an aircraft door either, but he was just doing his job. She held out her arms and he ran the sensor over her sleeves, her back, her front, shoes and inside her handbag.

While they waited for the sensor machine to

spit out the verdict she asked, 'Do you know how far away Gate Sixty-One is?'

He nodded to his right. 'Seven minutes that way.'

Good grief didn't begin to cover that.

'Clear. Good luck.' His tone said she had little chance.

Isabel ran. Saw a sign directing her right. Kept running. Saw another sign and kept right. Ran. Puffed. Felt her chest tighten with the effort but kept on trucking.

Who knew she could be so determined?

There it was. Gate Sixty-One. Her footsteps slowed. No passengers. One cleaner emptying a bin. No flight attendants. The door was shut. The sign said *Flight Closed.*

A sob burst from Isabel's mouth. She flopped into the nearest seat, head bowed, and sucked badly-needed air into her lungs. She'd actually never thought she would miss that flight. She'd thought she was meant to be on board. With Dom. Surprising him.

Now she felt like an idiot. A prize fool.

Embarrassed by the whole idea of chasing the one that got away.

She pulled her drink bottle out of her bag, but it was dry. Not even a drip. She'd had to tip out the last water at the last security check. This sucked big time.

Isabel drew in a long juddering breath and stood. Walked to the nearest bubbler and filled her bottle. After a long swallow she let the tension of the last four hours gurgle down the drain with the stream of water.

She'd tried. What more could she do? She'd fly home. Maybe stay the night in Coffs Harbour.

Except her car was at Port Macquarie, not Coffs Harbour, and she didn't know the town. A dingy hotel would do her in. Best make the almost three-hour drive home.

Heart in her shoes, Isabel walked slowly back through the terminal, not even sure how she went from Departures to Arrivals in this terminal.

Who knew?

She'd never missed a flight before.

She'd never chased a man before.

She really should let Faith know what was going on, which she hadn't earlier because there'd not been a spare minute between all the deciding and rushing and running.

She drew her mobile from her bag and pressed the number for her niece. 'Hey, Faith.'

'Isabel, where are you? How are you?' Before she could answer, Faith went on. 'You sound strange. Dom told Rai you should have arrived home hours ago.'

Did he? Well, she guessed that was the impression she'd given. 'Long story. I'm at Sydney Airport.'

'Sydney?' A pause. 'Oh, my,' Faith said softly. Incredulously. 'You followed him. You're going to Italy, aren't you?'

No one said her niece was slow on the uptake. 'That was the plan, but I missed the flight to Rome. Now I'm just sitting here, wondering what to do next.'

'Um… Izzy. Darling Izzy…' Now Faith sounded strange.

'What?'

'Dom's not on that plane either.' Faith sounded breathless with excitement. 'He's flying back here.'

Isabel stared at the phone for a moment before lifting it back to her ear. 'What flight number?'

'QF2164. Leaves at fifteen-forty.'

Her chest faint with growing excitement, Isabel stood. Started back the way she'd come with renewed purpose. 'Faith, I have to run. I'll call you later.' And she hung up.

Dom glanced out of the window to the woman striding across the tarmac towards his aircraft and his breath caught in his throat. 'Isabel…' he breathed. Her hair flowed behind her, her chin tilted up to the aircraft, long steps decisive.

Disbelievingly, joy-filled, he savoured the side angle he had of her face as she entered and greeted the hostess. Showed her the boarding ticket. Then she stood for a moment at the front of the cabin, scanning passenger faces.

Her search skimmed over his and swung back. Their eyes met, held, locked and Dom's heart soared and his eyes widened. She'd come to fly with him. His brave Isabel had been coming to Italy.

The hostess spoke to her.

Isabel smiled and nodded and she looked back at him to wave her boarding pass. All he could do was stare at her incredulously with sudden joy bubbling up inside him like Vesuvius on its most spectacular day. They would go together. On the next flight.

Dom's hand flew to his seat belt and unclipped it. He rose, and in his haste almost hit his head on the hand luggage compartment. He ducked away.

'Isabel…' His voice came out hoarse, exultant, uncaring of the faces that turned to him as he slid from behind the seat and closed the distance between them.

Took her small, precious hand in his larger one, looked down at her fingers curled in his briefly in disbelief, and then back at her face. She waved the boarding pass under his nose.

His other arm slid around her and he squeezed her to him before he let her go. Indicated with his head towards the door she'd just entered.

'You won't need that pass. We're flying to Italy.'

EPILOGUE

One year later

IT FELT AS if Isabel had been waiting to share Christmas morning in Lighthouse Bay with her husband for ever. In two months it would be their first wedding anniversary—so only a year—yet so much had happened.

Apart from falling more in love every day, sharing a joy in each other's company that permeated the solid relationship between them, they'd travelled through Italy for a month after Dom's business had been concluded, and then home to a beautiful Lighthouse Bay wedding organised by Faith and Rai in their absence.

They'd just had their honeymoon first.

The factory site in Florence and new build had been sold, the Villa Salvanelli had been left with a skeleton staff to maintain it, and they'd shipped Dom's personal belongings to Lighthouse Bay.

Since then, they'd settled into Isabel's little house and her husband had eased into working at the new medical centre with his brother. The town was delighted to have two new doctors open for business.

Dr Reg had retired, both he and Myra happy he was no longer leaving the hospital short-staffed.

Isabel had even done a few shifts at the cottage hospital after a refresher course in midwifery and general nursing that had brought unexpected satisfaction to her heart.

But now everything had changed.

Changed by an unexpected missive from Dom and Rai's family priest in Florence and a whirlwind of twin country organisation her husband had managed with remarkable ease considering the legal red tape.

Two toddlers, two years old. Twins. A boy and a girl. A crazy, tumultuous, terrible two of toddlerhood had flown home with them a month ago on an epic flight with two fractious children, and Isabel and Dom, despite the culture shock, couldn't be happier.

Matteo and Bianca, sudden orphans, distant relations to the Salvanellis, with no closer family able to take them, had come to live in Lighthouse Bay with her and Dom. First, they were fostered and later the adoption would be finalised.

Isabel placed the small Santa sack at the bottom of one bed. Bianca, deeply asleep, the older by half an hour, was a strong and boisterous child who looked after her brother even at that age. The dark-haired little girl bossed Matteo yet was the first to run to him if he cried, her bright eyes observing her surroundings and learning quickly to understand the language of her new mother.

Isabel carefully placed the other sack and decided their new son was near to waking. While the more timid of the two, Matteo, slower to talk and slower to cuddle, shared everything from his sandwich to his toys with his sister and looked to her for guidance in their new world. His eyes followed Dom when he passed, and for the moment Dom had more luck in making the child smile.

But they'd get there.

Early days yet. And she remembered a time when she'd said to Dom that God's plans could not be understood by mortals. She could only be thankful for this grand plan.

Now, with the dawn light painting pink across the clouds out to sea, Isabel looked across to the two miniature beds in the corner of Chloe's old room. These two small children had come into their life and already given them so much joy and love.

The new house plans had been submitted to join the house next door to theirs in a renovation to rival his brother's across the road. Their house would grow more crowded as the children grew and Dom had snapped up the premises when it had gone on the market before Isabel had realised what he was planning. Apparently, he could be as impulsive as his brother.

She heard Dom's footsteps behind her and he rested his hands on her shoulder as he leant down to nuzzle her neck. 'All my love to you at Christmas, my wife.'

She turned in his arms, reaching up to touch the glorious stubble on his chin. Feeling the warmth of his mouth and prickly chin as he turned his face to kiss her palm. Heat sizzled through her in this now accustomed storm of lightning strikes she'd never known existed.

'And to you, my love,' she whispered, not to wake the children. 'And our first Christmas with Bianca and Matteo.'

'We are blessed. Let's sneak back to bed before our children wake.' His laughing whisper was warm in her ear, making her skin tingle and her mouth curve. 'I have something for you for Christmas that requires privacy,' he murmured.

She didn't like his chances and laughed. 'We could try.'

Holding hands, they turned and began to tip-toe out of the room.

* * * * *

If you enjoyed this story, check out these other great reads from Fiona McArthur

Second Chance in Barcelona
The Midwife's Secret Child
Healed by the Midwife's Kiss
A Month to Marry the Midwife

All available now!